Damn Boy George & Thanks for the Heartbreak!

A Novel By Nolli

WRITTEN BY
MAURICE "NOLLI" RUBIO-MCMILLON

EDITED BY MAX HODGE

ISBN 979-8-9884272-0-9

For Mary Florence Apeler-Black
(1930 - 2022)

You showed all of us the transformational power of unconditional love, and with all my being I'll burn bright into the night as an example, that all the world may see and know.

Damn Boy George & Thanks for the Heartbreak!

ACKNOWLEDGEMENTS
Praise be to God!

For the beautiful life that you provided to me, in raising me to be loving, compassionate, and truthful, to have humility and to seek moderation in all things – I thank you, John W. and Mary F. Black, my adoptive parents. You will both forever be missed by those of us left drifting in your wake.

My life partner, Manuel Rubio-McMillon, I thank you for the daily love and inspiration that you give me. It sustains me and gives me shelter from the tumultuous circumstances that life brings. We compliment each other in the only ways that truly matter.

My sister, Roxana Vega, I thank you for providing me with the comfort that comes with knowing that I am not alone in this world. You are my favorite person because you see the world as I see it, but you deal with it in such a magnificently adult way that I can only admire. Everyday I am more and more thankful that I was blessed with you in my life, sister.

Alicia Vega, my biological mom, who became my best friend and stepped back into the role of mom after years of separation. No one I have met or known, has changed their life in as dramatic a way as you have. Neither has anyone lost as many loved ones. Despite the losses, your ability to move forward with love towards others is more than an inspiration. It's the very core of what it means to be compassionate. Alicia, you are a saint–the world just doesn't know it yet.

A special thank you to my cousin, Calvin McMillon. He's the first writer in our family that inspired me to take up the craft and seek satisfaction through all the means that my spirit yearns for.

Boy George – Thank you for just being you. You lended me and countless others your courage in the face of bigotry, exclusion, and hate. Damn you for the cost, but I graciously thank you for the reward that it is to stand and proudly say, *I'm gay*.

Lastly, an acknowledgement to the person I wrote this story to reach. In memory of the person you were before, C.A.S. I've never been the same since our friendship expired. Writing this was the next best thing to closure I could come up with. You were such an incredible force in my life; one that forever marks me.

We say we love someone, but how can it have fidelity in a reality where we both exist as strangers. True, unconditional love isn't convenient. If you can just drop someone out of your life, then that word should only ever leave your lips followed by the conditions that it carries. Otherwise you've made yourself the monster of someone else's tragic love story.

This is *our* story.

I doubt you'll remember me – that's ok. I remembered enough for the both of us, and I did my best to capture all the details as I relived our story one last time.

With this, I lay that version of you to rest in my memory. With this, you're forgiven, and I am haunted by the ghost of you no more.

Ashes to ashes.
Dust to dust.
I love you.
I miss you.
Goodbye.

CHAPTERS

PREFACE
A Good Night for Heartbreak

The sky is beautiful tonight. It reminds me of a navy velvet lined box containing scattered jewels that shimmer with all the colors of light. The kind that sparkle best against a dark backdrop. A warm breeze hinted with a cool current swirls around mimicking my place here tonight and my internal state. The coolness hints at a thunderstorm, somewhere out there in the night. Unseen, unheard, but felt. It electrifies the air, which already carries the emotions of strangers that pilgrim to the edge of the water across from the hall.

I watch them glimpse down at their reflections, caught off guard by the sight. The water draws me nearer, I feel summoned by the sounds and scents of waves crashing against the rocks, spraying salty water into the air.

The mist is a child born of conflict between the water and the earth; the moving against the immoveable. As dark as it is, I peer into the water to see myself – childlike. I appear like a specter on the surface of the water, backlit by the ambient lights of far off lamps and burning stars further away than I can imagine – yet, there they are, close enough to nearly touch.

Am I smiling or frowning? I can't yet decide...

At long last, I have let go of a person whom I loved, unrequited, and was abandoned by. At last, I am healed from the deepest wound I have yet known; inflicted by someone I whole heartedly trusted with my soul. The water calms for a moment, allowing the reflected image to become clear and focused.

Ahh. I see, now.

He smiles. He smiles, and I realize he is not me. He is the boy I knew, forgiven this night through love, pain, and... reflection.

He is you.
You are me.
And tonight, we are healed.

CHAPTER 1

ONLY

The wine in my stomach sloshes back and forth, nauseating me as I monitor the MC that tramps toward me. He's been making his rounds as artists arrive, pressing us to introduce ourselves on the microphone so that we don't take up *too much* time during the auction.

The MC is a man named Christopher *something*. I should know this, but I don't pay much attention to local politics. He sits on the board of county commissioners, a role he picked up after he broke his leg at a dance competition. I heard through the grapevine that he was an awesome professional dancer and choreographer, but his injury cost him his career. Since then, he's become an active guardian for the arts in our community, taking up a position to ensure that the arts remain well-respected and funded. Something that we have needed for a while, since the last major arts organization collapsed from financial mismanagement. That's the politically correct way to say that the director embezzled all the cash.

That bastard.
Sigh. He's about to call me out – I can feel it.

With each step he takes closer, my heart jumps, my hands dampen, and my eyes glaze over as if I'm about to cry. It's like my body has an aversion to any chance that I get a mere 15-seconds of fame.

Heh. A smirk crosses my face and breaks my anxiety.

15-seconds of fame.

Growing up in the 90s, the saying used to be 15-minutes of fame, but people's attention spans have shortened so much in the last 20 years that 15-seconds is all you get now. And yet – even that is more than I can stomach tonight.

I push away from the table and lean forward in my chair, driving my elbows into my knees as my hands cup together over my face. I draw down to my mouth where they curl under my chin for my head to perch on.

Random thoughts storm my mind distracting me from the approaching MC.

> *I really shouldn't touch my face,* especially as my pores open up and sweat. I'll probably have a pimple tomorrow for doing it. Ugh, why do I even do this to myself? None of these people like my art! I'm just wasting my time and everyone else's. Is that a *Mochachino* handbag up for auction? Those guys have really been killing it. I really like that shiny buckle he has as a clasp on the bag. I wonder how he made that... like, did he hand make them or did he order them from China? I wouldn't mind getting to know them – maybe I'm better at fashion design and I'm missing my calling here...

The sound of the MC's voice breaks into my thoughts.

"Uh Oh!", the MC calls out.

I panic at the thought that he might be behind me, when I turn he is nowhere near me. *Whew!* I wipe my face with my hand and scan the room . Thankfully he's caught some other victim in his spotlight net. I can barely see who it is until she stands to introduce herself to the growing crowd.

"You all know *this* pretty lady!" The MC wraps his mic-less hand around the woman's back to her far sided arm.

She then squirms loose with a chuckle and playfully punches him in the arm as the attention of the room falls upon her. Her face awkwardly twists into a smile as the lights gleam off of her moistened skin.

She stands on the shorter side and is an older woman, though not much older than myself. She wears a *Lilly Pulitzer* styled dress with very bright and obnoxiously-neon colors that work well *for her*. She accessorizes with matching costume jewelry – the large, plastic type that reminisces of 60s mod fashion. Her hair is a cute, a shorter cut that's wide at the ends, and narrows at the top. It's wavy and looks crispy, like the noodles you add to your soup broth at a Chinese take-out joint. It's a pretty color too, a mix of brunette and blonde strands that compliment her copper skin tone. She's a rather beautiful woman and one of the best artists in our town.

I love being around her, she inspires me.

"Not that you *need* to, but why don't you go ahead and introduce yourself to all these good people, Nadia." the MC suggests as he hands her the mic.

"Hi there everyone! My name is Nadia Zayas, and I'm a local artist most known for my *colorful* mosaics. You've probably seen my work on many of the benches around town, and if you didn't already know that was me – now you do."

The crowd laughs as Nadia giggles following the comment. Our city commissioned her years ago to decorate over 40 concrete benches as part of a cultural grant they received. Nadia hosted a contest with the local high schools to create visuals that she would then craft into mosaic artworks on the benches. I was an art student at one of the high schools at the time, but I wasn't selected. This adds to my anxiety of being in her presence and feeling unworthy.

How could my art sit up there next to hers?

She continued to introduce herself, "I want to personally thank all of you for coming out and supporting such an incredibly important event. Tonight we're here to raise money for LGBTQ+ suicide prevention, a topic that is very personal to me. Not many people know this, but..."

Nadia's eyes turn red and gloss over quickly, her bottom lip also trembles. The MC places his hand on her shoulder to give a physical presence to his emotional support. The crowd falls silent as she gathers her strength and pushes through. The tears in my eyes that began as anxiety, dropped out of empathy – I already know what it was she had to share.

"I'm sorry..." She sniffles. "15 years ago, my little brother, Ramon... took his life. There is... no amount of time – whether a day or 10,000 days – that changes how hard it is to say those words out loud."

Nadia closes her eyes and tilts her head up to the sky as she takes in a deep breath, exhales, and reclaims her emotional strength. The MC's hand never leaves her shoulder, and she places her hand on top of his in a sort of gracious way to thank him. She exhales, focuses on the crowd, and begins again.

"Which is *exactly* why I'm here, giving my best to do my part for someone out there like *Ramon* to get the resources they need. Please, enjoy your night, bid high on all this beautiful art, and continue to support amazing organizations and artists who do the *good-work* in our community. Thank you all." Nadia pats the MC's hand, smiles at the crowd, and quickly turns to hug him before she takes her seat.

The MC assesses the crowd and looks to lighten the mood by reminding patrons and buyers of their drink tickets and tonight's sponsors. The MC scouts other local political leaders like the mayor and members from the chamber of commerce, and goes after them comically for donations and high bids in front of everyone. Meanwhile, Nadia leaves her table and retreats to the women's bathroom *probably* to gather her emotions.

This is a typical night at an art gala – we must share our heartbreak to capture the interests of buyers, and it is met with as much concern as a superficial greeting. Is this what it means to be an artist? To put our trauma and emotional scars on display so that our work is of greater value to these people whom look for nothing more than wall decor. Her art reflects the state she wishes to find, whereas mine dwells on the dark memories that entrap me. My heart aches for her loss, her grief, and her brother.

That could have been my sister speaking...

I wipe the tears from my face as anxiety trickles back into the forefront of my thoughts. I've contemplated my introduction at these charity events many times, but when the moment arrives that I'm in the hot seat, all my rehearsed lines condensate as sweat in the palms of my hands. I'm rarely prepared to stand and confidently announce myself as well as other artists do. Especially like Nadia just did.

How can I follow that?

She definitely did it right, certainly years of practice at allowing her challenges to inspire buyers to open their wallets. The raw emotions behind her words were enough to move me to tears and even make my cheap ass want to buy everything up there. I guess I could share my own personal battles with depression, but now it seems like I'd just be attempting to top Nadia, sharing it feels disingenuous at this point.

Ugh! I should have gone before her. I'm such a loser...

I survey the rest of the art on display and pause at mine. It is a digital piece, printed on metal that's very large and framed. Digital art is still controversial in my town, so I usually enhance my pieces with some 3D sculptural elements— not this one. It's composed of layered images that I photographed, everything from the background textures to the portrait of the boy that the piece is built around. My composition is arranged to create mystery, pull in the viewer's eye and question – *who is he?* Like most of my art, it uses dark colors, like purples, grays, and blacks with hints of pinks and teals.

The boy's expression though... it's expressive... it's provocative...

It's so out of place here! What was I thinking submitting such a riské piece for a suicide prevention event?! I should run up there, grab it, and ditch. So embarrassing...

I drop my head into my palms and feel the shock of a hand as it lands on my shoulder. It's small, but warm and guides me back to this captive moment. The hand belongs to my sister and I turn ever so slightly to face her, fearing that it's my turn at the crucible.

"I *think* he's about to call on you, brother." Elle whispers to me.

Greaaat.

I feel the blood drain from my face as more beads of sweat form across my body.

I'm gonna be sick.

Hah. "Are you OK? You look a little *nervous.*" She notices and chuckles at the sight of my anxiety. No doubt, she enjoys my struggle. I'd laugh too, *if I could.*

"I honestly don't know why I do this to myself. I hate formalities, I hate putting on a show, and I *really* hate having to dress up. I should have stayed home," I tell her as I adjust my shirt to pick it loose from my dampened body. My clothes always cling a little to my body, but never more than when I'm nervous. The shirt suddenly feels skin tight, and I am severely uncomfortable in it.

"Nonsense." she says, "You've worked hard and deserve to bask in your moment of fame. Take it…", she whispers with a smirk, "bitch." Her glass of wine drifts up to her face and she sips it through a golden metal straw that she brought with her.

That's my sis, bougie as hell but sippin' wine through a straw like a grape juice box.

Her presence lightens my mood and eases my anxiety, something that not many people can do for me *anymore*.

"Ya know what, I think I need to refill my drink, so yeah – I'm gonna go do that." I state as I scurry up from the table seeing the MC making his way to my side of the room. Before I could take a step though, Nico – *my husband*, snatches the glass out of my hand.

"Don't worry! I've gotch'ya!" he yells and saunters off between the crowded tables in the hall. My mouth drops in shock at how quickly he appeared and disappeared again with my glass. My sister covers her mouth with her hand as she laughs, enchanted by my circumstantial confinement.

"You're not going anywhere, brother. Have a seat." She gestures with her hand for me to sit back down.

"Damn him." I state plainly, plopping back down into my chair. My sister laughs as she continues to sip on her wine.

Thank God for my sister being an equally introverted human being to keep me company at these things.

My husband is a social butterfly that knows everyone and their brothers, sisters, cousins, parents, grand parents, teachers, coaches... just, everyone. He's been all over the hall mingling and rubbing elbows with the elite, leaving me to my own misery, though I don't blame him entirely.

I'd leave me too, if I could.

"Brother, did you know that Nadia had a brother that committed suicide?" my sister questions.

"Honestly, I don't know much about her. I've only interacted with her here and there at these kinds of things." I reply.

"I wonder if he was gay, too." she asks.

"Well... *this is* an LGBT event, sooo that *might* be a hint." I sarcastically offer as she glares at me with a deadpan face.

"I can vouch for one thing though, it was way more difficult 15 years ago. Would have been nice to know someone else that was gay back then. Gay *and* functional, I mean." I tell her.

"*Gay and functional?*" she asks me.

"Yeah. Ya know, like, *not* crazy. In my early days, everyone I met that was gay was... well, they were just a little *out there.*" I add, but her expression becomes more confused.

"Eh. It's hard to explain. I guess *maybe* because we kind of grew up having to lie to ourselves and then the world it sort of *twisted* us and the way we interacted with each other. It's not so bad now, though. We're *normalizing.*" I try to explain my ideas better.

Growing up gay, mixed, and *somewhat* adopted in a small town of Florida was a terrible combination for any time period. I think that my circumstances made for a rather interesting perspective when discussing hardships, discrimination, and isolation. Nadia was older than us, I assumed that her brother was also older than us, meaning that he probably grew up in the late 70s or early 80s, following the Civil Rights Movement and Stonewall Riots in the 60s. He would have grown up in a totally different America than what I did. We can live in the same place, at about the same time, and yet *be* in totally different worlds.

Where in the hell is my husband with that damn drink?

I see a smile spread across my sister's face as a hand clamps onto my shoulder and startles me. My mouth salivates for the liquid courage I desperately need, but it was too late.

Damn it. I'm up.

Ahhh. "Here's another one that doesn't need much of an introduction! The new kid on the block that has everyone talking, Sid-*vicious*!" The MC announces to the crowd as a rumble of laughter trails his words. I feel his hand tighten on my shoulder as a confirmation that he's warmed them up for me, but as I take the microphone I can't stop the curt sarcastic giggle that pops from my mouth when I correct him.

Uhuh. "It's just Sid, actually." I glance at my sister who giggles under her breath at my frustration.

Why am I always the complicated guy?

"Good evening, everyone!" My voice instantly creates feedback on the microphone. I'm accustomed to having to really push my voice out for people to hear me since I'm a low volume kind of guy, so without thinking, I did just that. My eyes scan the room for my husband and catch him at a table with cupcakes chatting up a couple of old women – *two* of his favorite things. Seeing him helps me muster my courage to speak, in the absence of alcohol. I pretend the audience is him and it loosens me up.

I look at the mic as if it had grossly offended me and speak *to* it as though it were a member of the audience. My entertainer side kicks in and the show begins.

"I'm not *vicious*, really," I say to the microphone. The crowd of patrons, most of whom are old enough to get the reference, burst into laughter. I have won them back with a quote that builds on the MC's mockery of my name.

Damn him.

That's my personal catchphrase tonight, I can feel it.

Hheh. I nervously laugh. "I'm no rockstar, not by any stretch. I was born and raised here in Fort Pierce – an actual Florida native – rare, I know." The crowd chuckles as I hear small conversations start to spark up regarding where various people were transplanted from.

I'll use that.

"When people see my art style, they usually think I'm from a metropolitan area like Atlanta or New York. I bet a lot of you are from *Long Island*." The crowd responds with laughing and I see fingers pointing at one another while opposite hands clutch their drinks.

Good, they're relaxed.

"Yeah, I thought so." I do my best Long Island accent, "Not for nothin', but you can definitely hear it in the accents and see in those accusatory fingers you're all so well known for, right?" The crowd laughs harder and I spot someone in a dark corner who throws a middle finger up.

Perfect.

Ah! "There'tis! That's the finger I was talkin' about!" I point out the stranger in the dark and laughter roars across the hall as the audience focuses on the finger and reacts with more middle fingers in the air.

In the last couple of years that I've gotten more involved in the arts community, especially these charity gala events, I've learned that these events are less about the art and more about participating in an alcohol-induced social activity.

Oh – And the tax write offs. Definitely a lot of those.

"Alright – 'nough of that." I gesture with my hand to cut it out, using the last of my will to continue the accent.

These people don't care who I am or what I'm about. They want what all people want – to be the subject, made to feel important, and given a superficial reflection of their own lives. Yet, I still try. What a fool, am I.

"On a serious note, I'm most inspired and motivated when I create something for a higher purpose." I pause and swivel towards Nadia sitting at her table. Her eyes have locked onto mine, and gloss over anticipating my words of acknowledgement.

"What purpose is there greater than the preservation of life? Earlier Nadia shared a story about the loss of her brother, Ramon. It's unimaginable. I can't fathom a day in this life without my sister – and my heart goes out to you, Nadia. You couldn't have said it better – no matter a day or 10,000 – those kinds of losses stay fresh and we, those left in the quake of such decisions, are forever affected. I hear people often ask how anyone could commit such an act." I pause and realize what I just said and where the words may lead me.

Shit! Is this where I really want to go right now? Why'd I say that?!

The room fell unexpectedly silent and fascinated, waiting for an answer they've all asked a question to. An answer that I don't have. My husband has even stopped talking and eating – a *miracle*, and the women he was engaged with have affixed themselves to my words.

I am no authority on the matter... What the fuck, Sid? Did you really just do that to yourself?

I swallow down the anxiety that swells in the back of my throat to make space for my hallowed final remarks so I can sit down before the wine leads me to greater regret.

I've had my share of dark nights, and although I'm usually an open book, this isn't the place to tell my story.

"I don't know the answer to that, but as a deeply emotional being, I'd imagine those decisions come at a lack of feeling connected." The anxiety slides away from me. Good save, now give them what they want.

"Your attendance at this event and your ongoing support through donations, volunteering, and even the simple act of listening will save lives. For people living through their *dark nights*, what we do here tonight ensures an opportunity for a brighter morning." I managed to get myself out of the hole I dug.

There, I did it.

The crowd claps and the MC makes a grab for the mic. I hand it off with a curt "thank you" and quickly sit back down.

My sister looks at me in disbelief.

"For a minute there I thought you were going to take it somewhere darker, but you really drove that one home, brother." she tells me. "See – you were nervous for nothing."

"Yeah, for a minute there, I wasn't sure about it myself." I reply as I look for my glass. "Where the hell's my wine?" I whisper with frustration under my breath as I get more comfortable in my seat. My knees are weak from the adrenaline crash of being asked to introduce myself. What's worse is that during the auction I'll have to actually talk about the artwork I've submitted.

God help me.

Right on cue, my husband pops up behind me as a new cocktail floats from around my shoulder into eyeshot and lands in front of me. He places his hand on my shoulder and speaks into my ear so I can hear him clearly.

"So, they're out of Moscotto, but I got you tonight's special *COCK*-tail, *RedRum punch*." Nico whispers, emphasizing any words that are *dirty* sounding.

Gasp. I inhale sharply. "RedRum?! That's bad taste for *this...*" I try to hold in my laughter at the terribly dark humor in my mind.

"It *was* worse." he tells me. "I was talking to the bartender and she told me that they didn't know it was a *suicide prevention* event. She was told it was a Halloween thing, so they were originally going to offer something called a *Zombie.*" He giggles.

I move my hand to cover my mouth as I laugh, "Oh God, I don't know which is worse."

"She didn't either, so I told her at least with RedRum people may not get the reference." he continues and surprises me.

I didn't expect him to know RedRum from the Shining.

"I mean, it *kind of* looks like blood, but not really, right?" He tries to confirm my agreement with his thoughts.

Hhah. Wrong! – he doesn't know it either. Classic Nico.

"I almost forgot, these two lovely ladies wanted to come and meet you after they heard your introduction and I pointed out your piece." He motions the women to approach as he probes my eyes for irritation, ignores them, and taps me on the shoulder as he exits again.

Damn you, Nico.

I awkwardly rise from the table with my chair between us to shake the first woman's hand, but instead she knocks my hand away as she leans in to hug me as if we were long lost relatives. I can hear my sister snicker behind me. The second woman also prefers a hug and she leans in for one before I could reposition myself for a better embrace. I end up standing with one leg straight, foot planted on the ground as the other takes a knee in my chair. I hold on to the back of the chair like a child talking to adults.

This is lovely.

Up close, I realize that these are the two that I saw with Nico at the cupcake table. They both appear to be in their late 50s.

No. I'd say older, actually. My mom had me young at 16-years-old, and she's only 51 now. There's a greater age difference between her and some of her boyfriends than there is between us.

These women are probably a little closer to 60. One is short, round, and has a certain spunkiness to her. The other is tall, thin, and somewhat ragged. She looks like someone who has had a long and difficult life or smoked a few too many packs of cigarettes in her day.

Both women are wearing blue jeans, but very different tops. The shorter woman is wearing a very *comfortable* looking flannel button-up while the taller one is wearing a shear black blouse. They look as out of place here as my artwork does up there.

"Hi, Sid! So nice to meet ya! Your husband was just educating us about you and your art when we heard your introduction and were gripped by your words. You have a very attention-commanding voice!" the shorter one tells me while her friend nods in agreement. "I'm Michelle, and this my close friend, Becca." She puts her hands on Becca's shoulder and arm as if to present her to me.

"It's so nice to meet both of you. I'm Sid, though I guess you know that already." My introduction to them sounded so arrogant to me.

Could I be anymore awkward?

"Thank you for coming out tonight. What drew you to this particular event?" I recover by emphasizing their presence and motivation. Always a win, though its possibly a touchy subject for anyone since its an LGBTQ event and focused on the subject of suicide...

I should have chosen my words a little more carefully.

Without missing a beat, Michelle answers for the both of them.

Everyone's got that one 'crazy Michelle' friend, don't they?

"*Uh—duuuh*! How many amazing events do you know dedicated to the preservation of life? How could we not be drawn here? Like you said, there's no greater purpose." She says to me with such enthusiasm. Michelle has a bright, warm energy that radiates from her. It's infectious and reminds me of Nico. No wonder he was drawn to her.

Such... enthusiasm... If I've learned anything from Nico, its that when someone tries that hard for something, with such enthusiasm, it usually means something. The kind of something that carries a hefty a price. My heart strings are pulled and beg to explore the reason for such enthusiasm, but these events are often not the best place for such conversations. Or, maybe they're the perfect place and I'm not in the best mood. Maybe I'm never in the best mood, but my heart strings keep tugging for inquiry, though my mind is set on returning to comfort.

"Right! Have you both had an opportunity to check out all the artwork up for auction?" I ask and gesture with my hand towards the gallery to lead their eyes.

"Nope, not yet. We actually just got in before you started your introduction. In fact, I was *wondering* if you'd give us a personal tour of the works. It sounded like you probably know many of the artists on display and then you can also tell us more about yours. Nico told us a little, but he said he didn't want to steal your thunder." she insisted upon me.

Great... She got me. I bet Michelle dragged Becca here like she's dragging me to the gallery. Becca must be the type to not want to go, like me.

My husband does the same thing to me, taking me to social gatherings like game nights or couple's dinner dates.

If he didn't, I would only ever leave the house for art supplies.

We all need someone in our lives like that which is precisely why I married him. We compliment each other's strengths and weaknesses.

I wonder if that's the case for Michelle and Becca? I do get some lesbian vibes from them, but my gaydar is so gay that it has never worked on lesbians. It's strictly dickly.

I glance over to my sister who smirks and starts up out of her seat.

"Perfect! Sorry, hi! I'm Sid's younger and more beautiful sister, Elle. I didn't want to interrupt. Brother, I'm going to go get a refill while you take these gorgeous women on a tour." She pushes in her seat and cuts her eyes to me. I can read her eye lids like lips and they tell me, "gotch'ya bitch".

"Alright... yeah – let's go check out the pieces. To tell the truth, I haven't had a chance to look at all the art for tonight's event, so this will be new for all of us." I explain as I leave my chair of comfort and wade through the sea of seated people drinking and eating.

We reach the first work on display, a beautiful landscape by a well known descendent of one of the HighwayMen painters. The piece features a red Royal Poinciana, a common element in Florida landscape paintings, framed by a menagerie of green subtropical plants, all plotted against a vibrant sky of pinks and oranges. It was Sunset...

It's taboo for me to say aloud – especially living in the city where the last great American art movement happened – but I'm really not a fan of Florida landscapes. I grew up seeing them literally everywhere, and they always looked indistinguishable to me. Palm trees, poincianas, the St. Lucie River, the Indian River, estuaries – boring, all of it. In college I had to take an art appreciation class that required us to visit the local A.E. Backus Museum and Gallery, explore the current art exhibition, and write an essay analyzing and critiquing a piece that spoke to me.

As it so happened, the only pieces on display when I went were Highwaymen paintings of Florida landscapes. I found a particularly stormy looking one, fell in love with it's congruence to my own stormy nature, and wrote about it. Naturally my interpretation of the piece did not meet the instructor's idea of what I should have seen and so I received a "C"; which is pretty much how I felt about landscapes anyway.

"Tsch", Michelle sucked her teeth at the piece with a sort of wonderment. "It's a sunset. How beautiful."

I try to hold back an automatic eye roll as I lean in and examine the painting closer, giving attention to it's color and texture.

Fitting, they partnered such a beautiful day's end with such a melancholy event.

Becca leans in to pay her obligatory view to the piece. I observe her eyes scanning the the painting's surface, her mood tinting the entire view. Her eyes reflect the vibrant sky, dappled with clouds heavy with rain.

An art critic would delve into the artist's use of light, the juxtaposition of the vegetation to frame the tree in the clearing, and would certainly highlight the texture created in the piece using the palette knife technique. But I sense for you it's not about any of that, is it? It has some deeper meaning than just being a pretty sunset amid a coming storm. Is she on the verge of tears? I wish I had the courage to speak to her as easily as I monologue what I'd say or ask.

Her eyes cry for *connection*. I see them. I meet them. But I feel as hollow as the intent behind this painting clinging to safety, while yearning to be daring.

"Becca..." breaks from my lips; she is startled by my voice.

Too late not to ask now.

"What are you feeling about this one? Seems like you're feeling it." I unwittingly probe for my heart's satisfaction.

"Oh. Well, I like it. It reminds me of growing up here. If you've seen one HighwayMen, you've seen them all." She smirks and her tears recede.

I look around before responding to make sure no one is around to hear me, then I whisper to her. "You too, huh? We're definitely the minority here; being native Floridians AND not being obsessed with landscape paintings." We both laugh out loud.

Michelle is already at the next piece and is snapping photos of it as Becca and I stroll over. I explain to them that there are approximately 30 pieces on display and that the event usually has a theme, but this year's was open. Many of the pieces were extremely diverse from each other as a result.

"Ok, so – when I'm at events like this, I *never* use a person's real name to refer to their work if I'm being critical. You never know who's listening. I learned that the *hard* way. Instead I'll assign them a code name or use something from their art as a reference." I explain to the ladies as we tour and critique the pieces.

I introduce the ladies to each piece, sharing what little knowledge I have on each artist, their style, material choices, and whatever juicy gossip I could remember. The tour that I wanted to avoid brought all three of us laughter, tears, and enjoyment; I'm happy to be a part of this for them.

"Check out that one! It reminds me of some art from the 60's. Good times..." Michelle yells out.

"Oh *yeah*... 'tiki lady'," I reply. "I like her work. It definitely reminds me of *lowbrow* art which actually started in the 60s. In fact, it was commercial artists that wanted recognition and value for their art in the fine art world that were rejected and began the movement. Yet... Ironically, 'tiki lady' here came after me once at another event. She asked me about my work and what I did for a living. I told her I'm a *graphic designer*, and she said to me, '*Oh*. It shows.' As if my work had less value because of it..."

"That 'tiki *bitch*'!" Michelle corrects me. My mouth spurts out a laugh unexpectedly.

As we approach my artwork near the end, my anxiety kicks into high gear. Making art is a very cathartic experience for me. It aids me in working through past emotional baggage and dealing with the ghosts in my psyche. I think of it sometimes in the nerdiest way, as if my mind were a 90s computer and past experiences were left over data bytes taking up space on my hard drive. Well, you'd have to *defrag* your computer from time to time to eliminate those left over bits, and for me that was the art-making process. I *defragged* my emotional trauma through creation.

Aha. "Here we are..." I tell the ladies, gesturing my arms to present my art. Michelle and Becca both approach the piece and examine it closely. Michelle is intrigued immediately by the words embedded in it.

Becca, however, stands back and cocks her head to the side. She approaches it closer and holds her hand out to touch it gently. She's *connecting* with it in the most literal way I've seen. She looks at it with a sort of familiarity.

A sound erupts from her lips like a gasp for air. "Oh. Look – he's a baby! Look how young he is... and the *expression* on his face. Wow. *He looks*... like... he was in..." Becca stops her comment short as she backs up and her hand falls onto Michelle's shoulder to steady herself.

I step forward to explain its details to them and ask what Becca saw, but I am quickly overtaken by the MC reappearing on the mic.

"Alright! Alright! Alright! Ladies and gentlemen it's time to get those checkbooks and paddles out! But, we live in the 21st century, so we also have Square, PayPal, CashApp and Venmo. We're prepared, ya'll!" The MC approaches the gallery front and blocks me from a clean exit back to my seat.

Son of a bitch, he trapped me. Damn it!

The sweat beads reform on my forehead as I sense the impending situation.

"Let's go ahead and have our artists do a quick soundbyte about their pieces, shall we? Before we begin the auction, go ahead and get your drinks from the bar and give a listen to the artists while you do it." The MC announces as he scans the room. "Let's see, let's see, who shall my first vict..." He stops his sentence short as he peers from his peripherals at me in the gallery behind him. I see his eyes upon me, his gaze magnified 1000 fold. Everything happened so fast, I was completely caught off guard.

He's gonna make me go first? Really? Uugggh!

"You! Sid *Vicious*! Let's start with you!" he shouts and points at me as all the eyes of the audience once again fall upon my trembling, nervous body. Michelle and Becca scurry off to avoid notice and leave me there on exhibition with a piece that I feel embarrassed by to begin with.

Just when I was starting to have a good time.

I take a deep breath and release a sigh as I take the mic from the MC and approach the hanging art.

"Hi everyone! I'm Sid... and *this*..." I use my left hand to gesture to the painting, "this is titled..."

CHAPTER 2

POSSESSION

"*...Culture Rebel*," I announce to the audience.

Ok... where to begin?

I tap on my hip with one finger from the hand that feels as though it's the only thing holding my body still and in place. "*Right* – so, this piece features lyrics embedded in it from the band *Culture Club*. When you look closely you'll see them as words that are barely legible. The words create a visual texture by being piled on top of each other, layering lines, characters, and meaning – all of which is jumbled and confusing because *life* is layered, jumbled, and confusing. I like a lot of texture in my pieces, which can be very difficult to achieve in digital imagery. Lots of image layering and contrast is necessary to make that happen."

I awkwardly smile and look off to the audience at my side as though looking into a camera and stick up both thumbs – "Thanks college graphic design degree!" The audience chuckles.

"Anyway, the lyrics were very inspiring to me. They came from the song, *Do You Really Want To Hurt Me*, which is practically emblematic of being gay in our modern day culture – that's a whole nother conversation though. At first listen, I disregarded this song as *'meh'* and didn't think much about it, but after deeper examination of the lyrics, I felt a strong, personal connection to them." I pause, and notice Becca at my side still staring hard at the piece. Her gaze projects a sense of recognition that is both humbling and inspiring to me as an artist. I step away from it and stare at it as though to examine and reflect upon it with her and the rest of the audience as I continue.

I point out a lyric I emphasized in the work, "Especially the bit about *'everything's not what you see'*. Nothing could be more true or relevant to the topic at hand tonight, could it? There are layers upon layers to who we are and how things affect us.

When some of us appear happy or even sad, that may only be a mask for the heavier truths that lie beneath the surface of our observable lives. The face of the boy that appears in *Culture Rebel* hopefully conveys this experience."

"He's young."

He was 15 that day.

"He's beautiful."

In a way that I never expected.

"...and he's lost, unsettled on where he belongs."

As am I, with him.

I take a breath and Becca inches closer behind me, her eyes catching light with their watery infusion of mixed emotions. Michelle rushes to her side and pulls her back. I hear them whispering, but I can't make out their words.

The audience is dead silent, awaiting my next words. "Every action he takes, every word he speaks, every moment he shares is an opportunity where he hopes to be found. He only knows one thing for certain..."

Then it hits me. For once, what they want to hear and what's plainly true are the same thing.

The best art is a reflection of ourselves – what we most desire, what we most loathe, what we most need to be told. The greatest of all our stories boil down to this...

"He wants what all people want; to be loved and accepted." I state proudly. The audience applauds as I nod my head in acceptance of their praise. "Thank you." I'd like to believe it's a mic drop moment, but in reality, I suffer a walk of self-appointed shame to the MC. I timidly mouth my final goodbye to the audience, *"thank you."*

"Wow, what an excellent start to the introductions of tonight's featured artwork auction. Give him another round of applause, folks! Thank you, Sid... *Vicious*!" The MC pokes at me again as I throw daggers with my eyes at him for altering my name the entire night. "Thanks for being such a great sport, Sid!" He offers an apology for being my adversary. I close my eyes and nod my head in acknowledgement and acceptance of his apology.

He moves on and calls for the next artist to introduce their work, "Next up, we have a visiting artist from California. Welcome, Jules!"

Thank God that's over.

I sip my watered down RedRum punch through a tiny plastic straw. Elle and Nico are both intensely listening to each artist present their work as I catch a glimpse of Michelle and Becca exiting the hall into the atrium. Michelle seems to be trying to calm Becca, but it's not going well.

I wonder what that's about...

I can see that Becca is discomposed, but Michelle exits out the front of the building. I feel my heart strings tug again and I let loose a sigh from deep within.

No. It's none of my business.

The feeling continues to flutter within me as though my sigh brought it to life. It moves from my stomach, up my throat and edges between the back of my tongue and my esophagus. Either I need to throw up, or *something* is powerfully urging me to interact and interfere. Either way, I'm *sure* the RedRum is to blame.

Becca exists out the backside of the building towards the riverfront.

Why am I compelled to check on her?

I quickly gulp down the remainder of my drink for an added kick to move, which is not an easy task for me.

I better not regret this.

"I'll be right back you guys." I say aloud to my crew as I push out from the table to go find the damsel in distress. I walk out to the atrium and smell the aroma of leftover food from the dinner earlier. It's being trashed by the caterers.

So wasteful.

You would think as artists that our plates would be comped, but nope. We have to pay the full price of $60 per plate. The thought crossed my mind to finagle some food from the caterer before they tossed it all, but I'm on a mission now. My hunger will have to wait for our usual post-event celebratory *Taco Bell* feast later.

I walk out to the back of the building. It's an absolutely gorgeous October night. The moon is full and bright, lighting the star speckled navy sky in the most magical way. There's a warm breeze that tempers the cool current around us, and the palm tree fronds vibrate the air as they catch the wind, creating a sound best described as a shower of wind rain. Frogs and cicada flies layer their bellows and buzzing melodies over one another. I close my eyes and smell the brackish water that smashes against the rock-littered shore below us.

Oh, it's such a perfect night.

I deeply inhale to take in all the feelings and sounds brought to me by this night. I open my eyes as I exhale and feel renewed and refreshed for the moment.

There's no better birthday gift than this. Thank you for the beautiful night, Yahweh.

Tears form in my eyes as the breeze kisses my skin. I don't know why, but nights like these just squeeze the emotions right out of me like juice from a lemon. I'm not sad, though I'm not particularly happy either. I just exist, walking a fine line between two halves; the sacred and the profane. The magical atmosphere of nights like these create conditions that emphasize a memory of love and loss simultaneously within me. Some things I've never escaped, but don't all too often visit either.

Loss is like an unused room in a house, if you're lucky enough to live in one with that many rooms. It's there, you visit it sometimes to clean and prepare it for visitors, but you rarely have a use for it. It just exists for those short visits. In my case it's more like a flex room. I create my art there, I write there, and sometimes I just stand there in the doorway and imagine the visitors that once graced it.

Culture Rebel was made there. In a way, it remodeled it too. *Expanded* it.

As my eyes adjust and I move past my own internal moment, I see the silhouette of a person leaning against a rail in the distance facing the moon and the water. A lit cigarette eerily glows in their hand by their side and lifts to their face. The fiery glow just barely reveals Becca's features.

Called it! I knew she was a smoker, and how melodramatic can you get?
This is Nico-level type drama-type shit.

"Hey." I offer as I near her, but she doesn't hear my soft voice. She really doesn't look like she wants to be bothered.

Maybe I should just leave, but... No.

"Hey, is everything ok?", I ask with greater effort.

She's startled by my voice and jumps up a bit from the shock. She turns quickly to see me.

Ahh! "My God – hunny, you scared me!" She takes an extra long drag on her cigarette, then throws it to the ground and stomps it out. "Hi. Yes. I'm ok. I just needed some... pollution, I guess." We both laugh. "I know it's a terrible habit, and I had quit years ago when I had kids, but... life, ya know?"

I nod in acknowledgement and agreement. "I get that. I drink." I respond and we both laugh again.

"This *night*, though, it's absolutely perfect, isn't it? I almost wish the event was outside so I could enjoy both at the same time. Ya know?" she says as she pulls out another cigarette.

"Oh yes! Good art, good wine, good night!" I blurt. We both snicker and she turns to look off into the night sky. I approach the rail to join her, admiring the starlit navy velvet above us. The moon's reflection shimmers on the surface of the Indian River and in the distance lights of condos dot the shoreline from the horizon into the sky above South Hutchinson Island. The echoes of kids running and laughing can be heard where we stand all the way from the pier near us below the large south bridge.

Many people go there to fish, drink beer, and chill out. Our town is small, but we're famous for fishing. In fact, we are considered the sailfish capital of the world, although I've never even seen one here. Most of our tourism is centered around huge fishing tournaments and off-shore boat charters.

When I was younger, fishing was a very large part of my life. Every summer we spent weeks back-to-back camping at Long Point Park in Sebastian. My family was fond of using custom cast nets, especially ones made for catching huge black mullet, aka the real chicken of the sea. When prepared right, it's the best fish there is – few know about it though, most people think mullet is just for bait because of their fishy taste.

There's a trick to getting rid of that taste... The last time I showed someone the trick was 20 years ago and he couldn't handle it, I'll never forget it.

"Not really my crowd. *In there*, I mean." Becca reveals. "Well, don't get me wrong. I've organized some events like this... for people, like them... but they're not *my* people, ya know?"

"All too well", I commensurate. If not for these events, I'd never see any of these people in my day-to-day life.

They're mostly old wealthy families that are still part of the 'good ole boys' network that still controls our town. I'm not one of them – though I was born into one of those families. Having a mixed kid in the family sort of changed their social status. As I grew up and observed the peculiarities of racism, status, and class. I came to understand what my existence did to my family and for a while it led me to a *dark* place. Now, though, I take back what I can from those 'good ole boys'.

"But, if they're going to put their exclusive privilege and money to work for causes that I believe in... well, here I am." I add.

"Same, hunny." She returns, then repositions her back to the moon and leans against the rail. A lighter suddenly appears in her hand. "Your art in there, *Culture Rebel*, was it?" she asks, then places the fresh cigarette between her lips and lifts her lighter to spark the end.

"Yes ma'am?" I question and confirm simultaneously. I'm used to getting attacked on what I create. Whenever I show a piece that I consider done, someone feels it's absolutely necessary that I receive their input about what I could do better or how I should try to make more money by trying whatever is trendy that day. For a long time, this made me an insecure artist. I'd see others receive nothing but compliments, while I received nothing but criticism. This moment felt like it was going in that direction, my automatic defenses are prepared.

She takes a drag on the cigarette, then lets her arm fall, pivoting from her elbow, where her other arm grips firmly.

"I think... I..." she pauses, closes her mouth and averts her gaze to the side.

Here it comes. My anxiety and insecurities flood my brainwaves.

"I feel like... I..." she begins again, then stops short of completing her sentence. Her voice is soft, like she's trying to understand what she feels as she's about to say it.

Oh my God woman, spit it out! Just let me have it already. It's nothing I haven't heard before, I'm sure.

"*No* – I know..." she pauses again, but her voice changes a bit in tone. "I absolutely *love* it." She finally releases.

Ok. That's new. Never heard that before.

I am both relaxed and vexed. The idea of a smile forms beneath my lips in the muscles that would form them, but my face does not move. I have never experienced this before. No one has ever said, *'I love it'* referring to my work. I'm not sure what to say, but waiting too long to say something would only turn this magical moment into an awkward one.

"*Wow*. Thank you. That's the best compliment I've ever received!" I excitedly express with matching energy and body language. Then, I remembered how she touched it and appeared to connect with it. I saw her eyes captivated and moved to tears. I recall her being pulled to it in a trance-like state. All of it begged me to wonder. "But... *why?*" My mouth reacted faster than my brain could choose better words.

"What a *funny* thing to ask." she chuckles as she takes another puff on the cigarette and looks at me sort of questioning my reaction. "You don't like compliments?"

"Well, kinda. *Yeah*, I guess so. But, I don't know. I feel like *Culture Rebel* is a little out of place here. A little *too* provocative for this event. So, for you to say that you '*love it*', I can't imagine why."

"No – *yes*, you're right. Its *very* out of place here. But I think that's part of what makes it such a great piece. In this situation, it emulates the feeling of being out of place, something that most of those people can't even relate to. Something that you and I, well, we probably share that in common." she explains. "When I look into that boy's eyes – Well, how do you feel about it?"

"*Me?*" I ask rhetorically and she nods sarcastically. "*I love it.*" I toss back to her. Her head pops back as if smacked by a laugh that catches her off guard.

"Of course you do." She says. "But *why?*"

Hheh. "The boy in the piece represents the inner child that we lose touch with through adolescence. He's a reminder of the innocence we lose or... neglect." I answer.

"Ok... I *don't* buy that." she states with a jerky reaction to my words. "I'll tell you why I love it *after* you tell me the truth." She attempts to strike a bargain as she drags another puff out. "None of the bullshit you'd tell one of the people in there - none of that. Floridan-to-Floridian, I want the truth. I want to know..." her words trail off as she looks past me, her mind wandering in a thought. She pulls her gaze back to me as she drops the cigarette and stomps it out, again, "– who *was* he?"

> *This is exactly what you dream of as an artist – someone sees you in your art and they want to know the real you because of it. And maybe, just maybe, by chance they're rich and want to support you.*

Who was he? Portraits are so commonly used in modern art to capture and celebrate the beauty of the human form, and to convey emotions, experiences, and ideas. Ironically, the conveyed message doesn't always relate directly to a particular model. In fact the model is usually irrelevant as patrons typically just embrace the surface beauty, and make up their own stories about them.

That wasn't the case with Culture Rebel. There was a hidden truth in plain sight that no one else noticed because no one else was looking for it. No one, but this stranger. Her interest piqued my own.

Why does she love it, and why does she want to know about the model? Who is she?

"That's a little more *complicated* for me to explain... but you've got a deal!" I exclaim with a smirk. Becca smiles back, and raises her eyebrows as her eyes dart behind me again. Nico and Michelle are walking together to find us. He has Michelle's arm locked into his as they both stroll hurriedly.

"There you are! I've been looking all over for you, husband! They're about to start the bidding, come on!" He yells at me as if I were standing 100-feet away, but I'm literally right next to him.

"Ok, ok. Geez. How many drinks are you at now?" I ask abruptly.

"Enough." he giggles back.

"Hey, Sid! Don't think that lets you off the hook about our agreement. Right after the bidding war, I want the full story." Becca shouts out as we head back to the gallery. "Who knows, I may even buy it." She teases.

I glance back at her over my shoulder with greater suspicion.

"She said she might buy it?!" Nico gets excited and turns back to yell at Becca. "Yeah, yeah – let me see that paddle up and *then* he'll talk."

"Nico!" I yell in disapproval.

"What, she's gotta give a little to get a little, baby. That's how the world works." he chimes back at me.

We re-enter the hall and take our respective seats. The MC has been briefing everyone on how the auction works; we missed most of his spiel before we got back inside. Though, I've been to these things enough times to understand how it works, – that, and I never bid... I mean I donated the materials and time to make the artwork, paid for a ticket to be here, and actually showed up. They've been given enough.

The MC goes into his *auctioneer mode* and an assistant brings forth the first item to be bid on for the evening. In years past at similar events, I have seen artwork go for as much as $700.00 USD. Usually not much higher than that though.

"Hey folks, you already know the stories behind each of these magnificent pieces, so let's not waste any time. I'm starting this bid at $200.00! Do I have $200? Yes! Ok! I have $200, do I have $250? Dr. Lee? Is that paddle up? No? Don't tease me, sir! Do I have $250? Right there in the green shirt, I have $250! $300?! Can I get $300? Yes! Perfect, now $350!" The MC quickly auctions off each piece, shouting numbers faster than most can perceive them as paddles shoot up and duck down with equal speed. He gets to the Highwaymen descendent's piece and the crowd goes absolutely wild.

Bids blast right past the usual $700 threshold and rocket to over $4,500.00. All the artists in the room look stunned by the intensity of the bids over this particular piece. There didn't seem to be any rational reason that the piece went for so much so quickly other than...

"Damn! Those drinks must have just kicked in for

real." My husband quips out to me. "*Shiiit.* They got money like that to bid, they oughta pay ya'll a 'lil somethin' somethin'.'"

He's *not wrong.* A little payment for the supplies would be much appreciated, but we do it for the higher good regardless.

The remaining artists, including myself, are eager to see what our work bids for following such an impressive show. The next piece goes for $2,000.00, but is donated back to the auction by the winner and earns another $2,000.00.

Insane.

Then the next goes for $1,600.00.

Incredible. Really.

These high bids continue on for a few more rounds until finally, *Culture Rebel* is up for bid. Nico, Elle, and I all sit on the edge of our seats excited to see what it earns.

The MC starts the bid at $200, but for a long while there are no takers. I scan the room and see most of the patrons are disinterested.

Fuuuck, that suuucks...

Anxiety begins to build rapidly within me as my embarrassment doubles for having provided an inappropriately provocative piece and for having been the stopping point for all these incredible bids.

"You've got to be *fucking* kidding me." Elle spews as she slams her wine glass down and raises her paddle. "These people are such assholes. You gave an amazing speech and that piece looks incredible. It's just 'cause you're black, brother. I hate this town."

I don't think I've ever heard her curse before.

Her words are quickly overshadowed by the fact that my own sister is having to bid on my art.

I'm a failure and she's right.

Being black means I earn less than other artists of similar style or caliber. It also doesn't help that we live in a beachy town that appreciates coastal art and decor while I provide art with an urban, metropolitan vibe.

"About damn time!" Shouts the MC looking at Elle, "I've got $200, do I have $250?"

A couple of men on the far side of the hall from us reluctantly raise up their paddle. The MC shouts again, "Alright, $250! Do I have $300?"

This painfully went on for a few more minutes until we reached $450 and the MC was about to close on the piece. "Ok, ok. I guess $450 is as good as we're gonna get. You guys got me all excited with those bids in the thousands, but I guess the alcohol's burned off. Someone get these people some more drinks, would ya? $450 going once. Going twice..." The MC was about to slam his hammer down when suddenly a paddle shot up all the way in the back of the hall, just at the entrance from the atrium.

It's Becca.

"$500?! Thank you Miss..." The MC trailed off as Becca over talked him with her hands cupped around her mouth.

"What was it that Sid said about a day or 1,000?" Becca asked aloud.

The MC wasn't sure what she was getting at, but Nadia stood up and walked over to him to take the microphone. She looked at Becca with a regard as though she knew her and repeated what she originally said. "Hi. Sid was referencing what I said earlier about losing my brother and *really* loss in general. Whether it's *one day* or *10,000 days*, it never gets easier. Let me know if you need to talk, ok?" Becca returns a smile to Nadia that confirms some connection, and an acknowledgement of some shared loss. Nadia hands the mic back to the MC.

"*Okaaay*, so we're at $500!" he begins again.

"No!" Becca yells at him. "You *heard* Nadia, Chris."

The MC's face twists up and he shrugs his shoulders unsure of what Becca means.

"$10,000.00!" Becca yells and as the number leaves her lips the entire hall gasps as everyone's eyes became affixed to her. "$10,000.00 and that young man buys me a drink!"

The MC looks over to me for acceptance, and while stunned I manage a nod with my head to confirm. "Well ladies and gentlemen, that marks the highest bid on piece in this hall – ever." He drops his hammer sudden and hard. "Sold for $10,000.00 and a *drink* to the woman in the blue jeans!"

My sister and Nico celebrate with the audience in an applause, as I make my way to the front, locked in step with Becca, for a photo. My eyes stay on Becca to decipher what this is *really* about.

"Congratulations, hunny!" She whispers. "I *can't* wait for that drink..."

Me neither, lady. I just hope that's all you can't wait for, cause that's about all I've got worth to give.

CHAPTER 3
TOO LATE

The auction tapered off with most bids returning to the norm, except for a high school student's work that went for $800. A part of me felt a little jealous that the high schooler earned higher than my piece could initially garner without the help of my sister, but it only reflected the truth in these events.

Year-after-year of participation has proven to me that works created by black artists earn half as much money as works by white artists. Of course, the HighwayMen are an exception to this and often incorrectly cited to discredit any racial biases. Quality of work, use of colors, title, composition, you name it - none of it matters once they introduce us and we're seen for our skin tones. I sometimes think it'd be better for the art if it was bid on blindly without knowing who created it. I'm sure it would make a major difference in the outcome; literally allowing the artwork to *speak* for itself.

A great example of this happened at tonight's bidding war. When I arrived, I saw crowds gathered around my piece on display. Other artists congratulated me on having made such a "magnificent work" – *their* words. They knew it was mine because they know me, but the patrons at these events only see us once a year or so depending on the frequency of the event. They don't see the incremental changes in our work as a result of our individual growth. They just see the art and see us.

The moment I introduced myself and was tied to *Culture Rebel* I killed everyone's vibe for it. It became taboo *with* me. How does *that* even happen at an LGBTQ suicide prevention charity gala?! How am *I* taboo *here*?! When I share my experiences, like this one right now, to people in my larger circles, they refute them as anecdotal and tell me it's just my *perception*.

> *Sure.* I get that. They believe my mind is wired to look for discrimination and so it finds it – I took AP Psychology, I understand the concept. But the thing is... I wasn't raised by black people that

conditioned me to look for unfair biases in white people, I was raised by white people who tried to shield me from racism until it became a topic we had to discuss. As I started interacting with people outside of my family in places like school or boy scouts or karate practice, I experienced clear and blatant racism.

The first time someone called me a *nigger*, I was 8-years-old in the second grade. It was an experience I will never forget.

Oh yes – racism for me started even that far back.

It was on a regular school day that we were lined up in a hallway on our way to lunch. I stood gleefully holding my first adult-requested, personal drawing. It was to be delivered to Ms. Litta when she had lunch duty with my class in the cafeteria.

A classmate in the same grade as me, Parker, was in line with his class passing us in the hallway when he saw the drawing in my hand. He snatched it from me, opened it up, laughed at it, then balled it up, spit on it, and dropped it to the ground as he looked me in the eyes and told me, "you're not an artist, you're a *nigger*". I immediately began crying.

Why would Parker do that?! I looked up to him as an artist. I respected him.

I didn't know what the word meant, but I felt his intent, which he accomplished; to use his power of position and authority to remove me from a title I sought; to keep me below him.

Parker was the prominent artist in second grade. His line work and shading skills were top-notch. Some even considered him to be the best artist in the whole school. Meanwhile, I was *just* beginning to take drawing more seriously. In between class activities, we had spare time to read, draw or complete worksheets – I chose drawing more and more, allowing my imagination to play all over the paper. My drawings caught the attention of other classmates and earned requests for specific characters from me. This eventually prompted a debate between classes about who the better artist was, me or Parker.

Over time, I was mixing the styles and details of characters, thereby creating more original looking ones. Thanks to *Sonic the Hedgehog's* relatively dark series airing at that time, I created *roboticized* woodland characters that influenced much of my work there forward.

My popularity as an artist grew, and other classes in our grade were sending drawing requests on notes through friends. I remember how I rushed to meet the demands, furiously drawing between activities feeling like a kid in a sweatshop to keep up. Only, it felt good to make something other people *wanted*.

However, this trampled Parker's identity as the top artist in our grade. Other students weren't asking *him* for drawings, in fact they never did. Parker was sort of a snob and didn't *play* well with others. I can't say for sure what emotions he felt, but he obviously felt something strong enough that he did what he did. Unfortunately for Parker, Ms. Litta was his aunt. When I made it to the cafeteria in tears and explained what happened, she was furious and took action that resulted in Parker being transferred to another school.

It took me 5 years to get over what Parker said to me. His words shattered my self-confidence, and led me to stop creating art that I shared with people. Something that I'm *still* dealing with at 36.

Discrimination is not anecdotal. Whether for the color of my skin or the *limp* in my wrist... People find whatever reason they can to put up a wall and exclude me and

others. Exclusion must *feel* good to them. There is
nothing I want for myself so much that it merits making
anyone else feel unworthy. I was raised *better* than that.

"Well – *that* was interesting." Elle states as she rises
from her seat. "Brother – congratulations! Sorry you
won't see any of that money though. At least you can *say*
that your art is now valued at $10,000.00! Becca did you a
great favor here tonight, she basically made you the top
artist."

Elle grabs her *Dolce & Gabbana* handbag as she
prepares to leave. She's wearing a cute white Spanish
blouse with a tan colored skort that she tugs down as she
stands.

> *I knew that blouse would look great on her the moment I*
> *bought it.*

Her gold earrings dangle and draw your eyes to the
golden strands around her neck. The jewelry nicely
compliments the light brown, nearly blonde streaks in
her curly, long hair. She's a work of art herself.

She inherited the best of our parents' traits; attractiveness, intelligence, and confidence – everything I lack. She received the best of their attention and intentions, being raised by our mom and co-parented by our dad when both of them were in better positions to be *actual* parents. She also experienced much less prejudice by being born nearly a decade later when mixed kids made up so much more of the population in our town.

"Right?! I'm really happy about it. But also, kind of shocked. My goal was to break the threshold I rarely get past, but now it's been blown out of the water." I share and wonder how it will affect my future.

"You mean... *Becca*, blew it out of the water." Nico retorts as he stands up and gathers cups on the table making life easier for the clean up crew. "Are we doing this drink now, or planning it for another night?" He asks knowing full well that he's ready for round two already.

"I'm guessing now. How can I refuse? She just upped my value." I tell him.

"No, no. I'm down. I'm just making sure. I know how you are after these things. I can smell the *Taco Bell* now." He giggles as he rubs his belly. "But I think tonight it'll have to wait 'cause you've got a date with Becca."

"Right. Maybe we can go somewhere that has food though." I assert.

"*Oooh*. I might join you guys then, 'cause I could *definitely* eat. How about that new place down the road, *Pickled*? I heard they have some really good food and drinks." my sister suggests.

Nico and I look at each other and speak in unison, "YES!"

Becca and Michelle are standing at the cash-out table where buyers pay for their artwork. Becca looks over to me and calls my name, "Sid!" She holds up the $10,000.00 check and pops it a couple of times with a big smile.

"Home girl must *really* want that drink, huh? I wonder if thats *all* she wants?" Nico snickers as the comment cracks my sister up.

"Nico!" she yells, "Don't make it weird for him!"

"I'm just saying, she dropped ten grand so you might have to put a little out." He laughs as he nudges my shoulder.

"Shut. Up." My sister deadpans. Then she bursts out laughing with him and further comments, "Ya know, he might have a point though. Maybe she's a cougar. You might have bitten off more than you can chew with this sale, brother."

"Nah, I don't think that's it." I detract from their battering of my good fortune. "*Something else…* is fueling this interaction, but I guess we'll have to get through it to find out what." Though, there is some doubt in my mind about Becca's intentions. Nico's jokes could be rooted in some possible reality that I don't want to become my own.

> *Why bid ten grand on a piece of art* asking for nothing more than a background story and a drink? Sure, it's a charity event with an admirable cause, but I don't know… That's a lot of money. She could have left it at $500 and still have been a hero to me tonight.

Mmhmmm. "Interaction. Yup." Nico chuckles. "With that *pussy!*" He whispers under his breath. My sister elbows him hard in his ribs as she covers her mouth with her hand to hide the smile cracking across her face.

> *Nico is 5-years younger than me* and in every way my complete opposite. I'm dark skinned, he's light. I'm average height, he's short. I speak one language, he speaks two. I climb mountains of adversity while

suffering a fear of heights, he sails seas of opportunities with the wind at his back. We help each other through this life. I keep him grounded, and he pushes me over my obstacles.

Sometimes he can be crass and a little inappropriate for certain settings, whereas I can be uptight and have a hard time being loose and wild. We help each other be our best selves in those scenarios.

This is one of those times.

I roll my eyes and give Nico a stern look. "Behave," I demand.

Nico straightens up and attempts to make a serious face, "Yes, sir." My sister's laugh is audible now. He mischievously grins at her.

Becca and Michelle approach us and I step forward to greet them, but Becca gets right to the point.

"Alright Sid, ready for that drink?" Becca asks.

"Yup. We thought maybe the new place down the way called *Pickled*?"

"Sounds perfect. We'll meet you all there." Becca and Michelle exit out the front as we follow close behind them.

When we arrive at the restaurant, Becca and Michelle are very impressed with the aesthetics. *Pickled* is styled like a modern farmhouse, with lots of black trim, white walls, light wood tones, and subway tiles. The lights hang from the open ceiling on large wood beams with a slight lean towards the industrial style that's been trending everywhere else for years. This hasn't caught on in Fort Pierce yet.

It's a busy night downtown, and the host tells us it's a 45-minute wait time for a table. I put Nico's name and phone number down to be called when the table is ready. Nico is the only one out of the three of us that would actually answer his phone, my sister and I only text.

We all agree to walk down the street to *Pierced Ciderworks*, a really cute cider bar that has an interesting mix of vintage motorsports decor that feels like a steampunk vibe. We enter without pause and find a spot large enough for the five of us. I grab a flight of 10 different ciders for the table to try and we make our way through the list. The table agrees that a coconut flavored cider, to our surprise, was overwhelmingly delicious. Michelle goes with Elle to the bar to grab another flight as the conversation moves beyond the alcohol.

Becca looks at me and Nico with a smile sprawled across her face.

The cider is working.

Nico is temporarily distracted by his phone, leaving me as the sole entertainer for the moment.

Might as well speed things along, I guess.

"So, what were you saying that you *loved* about the piece?" I ask casually, knowing it to be a fruitless endeavor. In part, it was an opportunity to move away from being any more vulnerable than I already was, but it was also a signal to her that she can ask now if she was waiting for a sign.

Uh-uh. "Not that easy. You show me yours, then I'll show you mine." she teases. Naturally, this catches Nico's attention.

"Wait *whaaat*? What are we showing? I wanna see." he interjects and we all laugh. "Don't get me excited for nothing."

Sigh. "Ok, but... you have to understand a few things about me first. If I just came out and told you about the moment I made the image, I would sound like a crazy, obsessed person. Which I'm not – I swear. Things are never as straight-forward as they seem. *Stuff* happens that complicates life and makes a mess of the simplest moments." I explain.

"Yeah, no. I totally agree." she says, then puts her hand out on the table in a display of openness. "That's exactly what I want to hear. What *happened.*"

"Alright." I confirm as I contemplate where to begin. "When I was in the 4th grade..."

Nico interrupts, "Holy shit, you gotta go back that far?! Daaaaamn!"

"*Yeah!*" I bark back with frustration. "Because the events that unfolded *then* had consequences that lead to this very moment now. So... let me talk, *damn.*"

Nico cowers. "Proceed, sir." he declares with a grin.

"Thank you..." I state. "...*bitch.*" I half jokingly poke at him. He smiles, straightens up, and puts his phone down to show that he's listening.

"As I was *saying*, things changed for me in the 4th grade... It was a distinctively bad year for me and my family. My mom was in a horrifically abusive relationship. My dad and I argued every time we saw each other. My grandparents – whom I lived with – began having significant health problems. And, I was experiencing my first crush which just so happened to be on my new friend, the most popular *boy* in our class, *Michael*. I didn't understand it at the time though."

"*Wait*, hold on, so why were you living with your grandparents?" Becca asks.

"When I was 3-years-old, my mom and dad committed armed robbery. They were sentenced to serve time in prison, three and five years respectively. While they were gone, my mom's grandparents took guardianship of me."

"Your mom's grandparents? So, your *great-*grandparents?!"

"*Yeah*... I usually just say grandparents to avoid the explanation, but *yes*."

"So, you were actually raised by your great-grandparents?" she investigates.

"Yep. I know. When I try to explain our family tree, I usually have to draw diagrams to show who raised whose kids, 'cause it's a tangled mess." I chuckle.

"But it is very *interesting*." She tells me as she sips down some remnants of one of the ciders. "Not a lot of people ever get to meet their great-grandparents. Even fewer would be *raised* by them..." Becca speaks as if in a trance, staring off past me. I look behind me to see what she's staring at.

"*Sorry*, just thinking out loud. Please continue." she tells me.

"*Right*. So... where was I? I ask and look towards Nico for direction.

"4th Grade, remember?" he sarcastically asks back.

"Oh yeah, *Michael*!" I start...

"*Michael*?" Nico questions. "You didn't meet *Mic*–" I jab Nico in the side with my elbow and sternly look at him with a death glare. "Oh! *That* Michael! Sorry! There have been *so many* in his life, I can't keep up."

"*Pay attention*, and you might! Anyway, before Michael, I never had a crush before. *Eer*, like a *real*, legitimate one, so the physical feelings that came with it freaked me out. I mean, I had the whole bit happening to me: butterflies in the stomach, blurry vision whenever I saw him, my face would get flush when he touched me... it was sort of euphoric I guess. But I also had some other side effects developing, the negative kind.

I was usually an outcast among the boys in school because I was so... *sensitive.* I feel like that was the 90s word for *gay.* I got bullied by a group of boys in my elementary school often which included everything from gang beatings on the playground to name calling and graffiti on my papers and notebooks. 'Gay', 'faggot', 'gaywad', 'Asswad' - that one made fun of my last name, 'Aswad, but you get the idea.

They called me these things, but I didn't exactly know what the words meant. We didn't use those words in my house. They were foreign to me, until I started feeling the effects of having my first crush. My mind was slowly realizing the connection between those feelings and Michael. What other boys described as the feeling they had in their bodies over girls, I was having over a boy. The words they called me meant to separate me from them, to make me feel inferior because my feelings were for someone of the same gender.

It created an anxiety in me that led to fear and self-hatred. The euphoria of being in love was overshadowed by stomach cramps, nausea, and a feeling of despair. I *blamed* Michael for my feelings, and started asking other students if they thought *he* was gay. Out of all the reasons I could give you *for* wanting to know, at the top of the list would be that I *wanted* to believe that being gay was infectious and that I was being infected by him.”

“Yikes. Your great-grandparents didn’t know what was going on?” Becca asks as my sister and her friend return to the table.

“Well, yes and no. Certainly they saw the depression in me, but I think they also discounted it as me entering my pre-teen stage of life. Later though, my stress manifested as physical problems for me.” I answer.

“Ya’ll look intense over here, everything ok?” Michelle asks, setting the new flight of ciders down on the table. “You guys ready for the next batch?!” She asks with excitement.

“Hell yeah, girl! Always!” Nico responds, grabbing one of the glasses immediately. Sid is diving deep into his childhood trauma right now, so perfect timing for the alcohol.” They all giggle.

“*Ha-Ha-Ha*! So funny,” I sarcastically fire back at Nico. “I’m just explaining the circumstances that lead to *Culture Rebel*.”

“Elle...” Nico deadpans. “He had to back to *the 4th grade* to do it though. Back to *Michael*.” Elle gives him a face and Nico replies to it with widening eyes. She catches on and nods.

"*Eewww*, bad year." she replies, shooting a look my way.

"Exactly." I add. "It's all connected. All those experiences lead here." I shuffle in my seat to get more comfortable and finish telling this segment of the journey.

"So there I was, questioning Michael's motives for befriending me, asking the opinions of my other friends. Which led to rumors that I was *telling* other people that Michael was gay, and I concluded in a confrontation between me and Michael. I apologized to him for the misunderstanding, but he hated me and wanted nothing more to do with me. Honestly I spent the next two years socially distanced from everyone as I tried to understand myself and continue to make amends to Michael.

He did end up forgiving me, but our friendship was never the same, in fact you couldn't even call it a friendship, but at least I was freed from my guilt.

In those two years I spent time alone writing my feelings and accepting that I was gay. I neglected new friendships and kept myself in a bubble to limit the number of variables that were affecting me so that I could be sure it was me and not some outside influence. By the time I was 12, I knew it was simply a part of who I was with nothing and no one else to blame. It was during that time that my mental health took a sharp decline.

I developed crippling anxiety and severe depression, both of which manifested as physical illnesses. I had nausea constantly, my stomach was always cramping and hurting me – this had my great-grandparents worried. They took me to doctors that looked for tumors, cancers, even severe brain injuries, and you know what they found?"

"What?" Nico asks. "Don't leave us hanging, *shiiit*."

Elle looks at Nico and rolls her eyes.

"Nothing." I tell them. "The doctors concluded that whatever was happening, it must be psychological. Fortunately, that wouldn't matter soon because my life was about to take another turn. By then, I was in the 6th grade and not well-adjusted at all. I was just about ready to start socializing again, but the anxiety kept me locked away within myself.

Also, and more importantly, I basically avoided any boy that reminded me in any way of the bullies from elementary school. Some kids from my previous school were at my middle school, and this meant I had some acquaintances, though I had no real close relationships with any one of them except for one girl named Kristal.

Kristal was my best friend in 4th grade and had been a major part of my life since the whole Michael *era*. We were friends that existed in each other's lives, but *just* kept missing each other until that year when we were confronted with one another serving on the school's safety patrol.

She helped me deal with my feelings and fears about Michael, unaware perhaps that I was gay and that part of my identity was emerging. She was the first girl I ever danced with, and everyone in my family believed she would be my first, maybe even my only girlfriend. But middle school changed all that. Maybe she began to resent me for not ever asking her out, or maybe she resented that I was *different*.

Upon our first few days in middle school she quickly demonstrated to me that I was at the low end of the popularity spectrum when I tried to sit with her at lunch. She *literally* put her leg up to block me and I'll never forget what that felt like."

Absolute betrayal.

"There are no friends in middle school, *just savages*." my sister pipes up. "I bet she still regrets that too, even to this day."

"*Maybe...* Today, she's the only active friend I have in my life from my school days." I add. "You get the social landscape though. Gay boys usually have some female best friends, but mine shanked me for the sake of popularity and I had no male friends that were close enough to even associate with – I was a complete loner.

"So then... where did you sit?" Nico asks innocently.

Good question.

"I didn't. I was too nervous to eat an actual lunch; the food in my stomach made me feel like I had to throw up. The only thing I could eat was a cookie, so I'd take my cookie and stand in the back of the lunchroom by an exit door." I shared.

"Wow. I'm sorry it was like that for you." Nico offers with a hand on my bicep. He squeezes it and smiles.

"Luckily, I found someone else in the same boat. A boy named Kris was *also* from my elementary school and *also* questionably gay, though he wasn't bullied for it like I was. He either pretended to be or was actually in fact oblivious to everyone *thinking* he was gay and worried about his social status by associating with *me*.

Mind you, this boy was way more flamboyant and *sensitive* than me, he was in orchestra – *take that as you please*, and he dressed super preppy. All that to say he had the classic markers of a 90s gay kid, but he *swore* he wasn't.

Anyway, we were friends by circumstance and since he arrived at the cafeteria everyday before me, it meant that I had a place to sit and not feel totally rejected. It was a turning point for me. I started to look forward to the lunch, because I had someone to talk to and relate to, even if he was super defensive around me. I wasn't so alone anymore."

Becca leans in closer. "Sorry, I just have to ask, is that him, in *Culture Rebel*?" she asks with a smirk. "It sounds like he probably came out of the closet at some point later in life. Did you two end up dating?"

"Me and Kris?! Hell no!" I respond. "There was definitely a moment once where I thought he and I might... but we had a falling out that crashed and burned our friendship. We're *OK* with each other now. We mended our bridge in our 20s, but haven't spoken since.

Some friendships are like that. They start and end

with very little reflection back upon them over time. Some run deeper and affect us in unthinkable ways. Kris and I were friends. I loved him as a friend and I appreciate the friendship he provided in my life for the short time he did. In fact, it was thanks to Kris that I met what was my last *straight* best friend."

Before I could continue, a vibration so loud it could be heard came from Nico's phone on the table.

Bzzt! Bzzt!...Bzzt! Bzzt!

Everyone pauses and we all look at each other, then at Nico.

Bzzt! Bzzt!...Bzzt! Bzzt!

He's unaware that the vibration we all hear is coming from his phone.

Bzzt! Bzzt!...Bzzt! Bzzt!

"*Uh?* You gonna get that, Nico?" my sister suggests. "Pretty sure that's our table."

"Huh? *Oh!* My bad, my bad ya'll!" Nico looks at his phone and confirms we need to leave. "Ooooh Yes! They're ready, let's go cause *this bitch* is HUN-gry."

We gather our stuff and make our way to *Pickled*. We're

greeted at the host's podium by a very handsome waiter who takes us to our table. We're seated and each begin to look over the menu. When the waiter returns, we order a pitcher of sangria for the table and our conversation continues.

"I'll take one of *that*." Elle states, pointing at the waiter. Everyone laughs, and Nico batts his eyes at the waiter's back just as he turns around to catch him in the act.

CHAPTER 4

HERE WITH ME

That's more like it.

I'm not accustomed to so much attention. It's nice, don't get me wrong, but... I'm not that interesting of a person. And I have very little practice telling my stories so I'm a better listener than a speaker. For this reason, I make an effort to escape the spotlight and move the conversation to Becca and Michelle. We really don't know anything about them. So far they've kept this conversation totally one-sided.

"So, Michelle." I acknowledge her while dropping my drink slowly to the table and lifting my eyes to meet hers. "Tell us a little about you and what brought you out tonight. I don't think I've ever seen you at any of the local charity art auctions before– not that I go to every one of them either." We all chuckle.

Michelle glances at Becca and returns her eyes back to me. My eyes followed hers to witness a hidden message exchanged between them. I glance over to my sister to enact the same and her eyebrows confirm she saw it too.

Who are you ladies?

"Well, actually tonight was my first time ever going to one of these events. I didn't even know they existed until Becca told me about them." she shares as she picks up her sangria and swirls it around. Michelle leans in closer as if to reveal some dark secret with her next words. We all lean in, compelled to listen. "And truthfully, *those* people are just a little too..." she pauses and looks at Becca, "what's that new word again?" Becca looks around as if she's trying to find it hiding somewhere around us.

My sister picks up her sangria holding it close to her mouth and sits back, "*Bougie*?" she offers. Michelle cocks her head to the side while raising an eyebrow. I snicker at her – those were definitely *her* people.

"Yes!" Michelle exclaims. "*Bougie*! Those people were way too bougie for me! First of all, I can't believe how much *some* of those people's artwork went for, especially the high schooler. I mean... high school art selling for hundreds of dollars? Really?"

I crack a smile, she steals the sentiment right out of my prideful heart, but she also adds to questions I have. "Yup. Here it's all about who you know, not the quality of your work." I agree and add to the fire she's starting.

"Well, that's true everywhere hun. Who you know takes you real far, real fast, or totally squashes you." Michelle goes on, "To answer your question though, years ago I used to work with a lot of non-profits as a grant writer. I like asking for money, but not dealing with those *'bougie'*-ass bitches." She cackles at her use of the word, we join her laughter.

"I moved here, to the Treasure Coast, in 1996 with my husband and kids. I got out of the non-profit game for a while and I've been jumping from job to job since. Right now I'm working for a bank in Port St. Lucie as a loan officer. I'm not satisfied with it. It's just... it's not fulfilling, ya know?

> I met Becca years ago when our boys were in little league together. She *was* a big wig with some local non-profits back in the day. She coordinated events like the one tonight, oversaw program

development, and *blah, blah, blah*. You get the point, anywho – she wanted me to meet some people, rub some elbows, and maybe get back into the nonprofit world – *which* I appreciate, but ya know what?"

She leans further in over the table towards the group as we huddle together to hear, "I'm just not sure it's for me anymore. I think I might be too old to keep up, ya know? I kinda want a simple, easy-going desk job where I can finish out the rest of my working years, retire, and enjoy old age refinishing cabinets and shit to sell at those big ass auction malls." Michelle laughs loudly as she imagines it.

"Yeah, I wanna be one of *those* old women. After visiting Fort Pierce a few times, *like tonight*, I'm convinced this is the hidden gem of the Treasure Coast. According to who you talk to, Port St. Lucie is the place to be, but it ain't shit. Every time I visit *here* I'm stunned at the beauty of this town. There's something magical here and you guys keep it under wraps very, very well. It's almost like Fort Piercians have convinced the world that it's a nightmarish hell hole. An unsafe place where there's nothing fun to do or nowhere safe to live... just to keep people like me out."

She falls back and cackles again. "But I don't blame you. I'd wanna keep all those damn jersey shore hos out too." Her smile quickly disappears and her eyes flatten, "Which I am not one of…" She continues, "I'm a *Long Island whore*." She simply states before sipping her sangria with a pinky out. She looks over to my sister and mimics her mannerisms by trying to sit up straight and cross her legs. She perches her cup just below her lips as though she were about to sip, but had something more imperative to say. "We're *classier*." she jokes as she flips her hair back with the most dramatic flair.

My sister lets out a bellowing laugh. "Yep, I see it."

Becca cracks a smile and snickers too. I think that's the first time I've seen her really lighten up this whole night, and now I know.

They're not lesbians, they're really just close friends.

Michelle is clearly a refuge for Becca, and probably vice versa. Friends like that are far and few.

"So, what brought you and your family to the Treasure Coast to begin with, Michelle?" Elle poses, intrigued by her story.

"Oh, simple. My husband is a carpenter. He came down here to help a friend out with some projects he was behind on and he refused to come back. So, I packed up the family and we all moved to Florida. Eventually, each of my sisters came down too–just before the housing market crashed."

Michelle continues "You ever see that episode of Oprah? The one where she's like..." Michelle stands up to reenact the moment from the show, "...'You get a car, and you get a car, and you! You get a car too!' Well, it was like that with housing loans back then. Anyway, they were practically giving them away to *everybody* without consideration to whether and how the loans would be paid back."

Michelle sits back down and continues, "Actually, that's how I ended up working at the bank. One of my sisters' is a loan officer, she recruited me because of my finance background. Basically, we had to clean up the mess that all the inexperienced loan officers made."

"*Wow*! I heard that the houses were *stupid* cheap after that. If I had the money back then that I have now, I would definitely have bought up several properties." Elle tells her,

"But, I was also only 14 in 2008, sooo…" she giggles.

Michelle's eyes widen as her mouth drops open. One of her arms extends, flying out as if to hold Becca back in her seat as a collision was imminent. "14?!" She exclaims, "14?! I thought you were only like 19 or 20 *now*. How old are you, hunny?!" Michelle demands. We all burst out laughing.

Elle has looked like she was 15 years old for 10 years since the day she actually turned 15. She doesn't look her age at all, which is true for all three of us. The age conversation always comes up and people are always astonished at how old we actually are. Either kids are looking older these days, thanks to their terrible diets and poor life choices, or we're incredibly well preserved.

The best example that I usually share with people is a situation that happened 5 years ago. Nico and I stopped by Target in Traditions on our way home from shopping at Bass Pro Shop in Port St. Lucie.

Yes – gay men shop there too.

It was about 9:30 PM, so we had time to stop and look

around. Nico liked perusing the office supplies while I would run all over the store from house decor to books to toys and clothes. We rarely made a lot of purchases, rather these stops were more aspirational for us.

When we walk up to the door we are met by an employee, which I assume is a greeter. I tell him *hi* and side-step him to enter through the door. Only, he side-steps with me and puts up a hand to halt me. He asks, 'where are you going?'.

Well, I looked around because I was *sure* he was talking to someone else. I definitely didn't know this guy – although admittedly I have a terrible time recognizing faces – so I continue to side step and he continues to block me. He asks me again, with more command this time, '*Excuse me*, where are you going?.'

I stop again and look at him to be sure that I don't know him and it isn't just some old acquaintance playing with me. I've given a bad reaction once in a past, similar situation and I regretted it. This guy was a stranger although, he was kind of handsome in this lighting.

'We're going inside to shop.' I tell him. Nico was directly behind me and nodded his head. The employee asks us, 'Where are your parents?' I look back at Nico, unsure that I had heard him right, and Nico's face lights up with the biggest smile that I'd seen in a long time. Nico spoke up to him, 'I'm sorry – *who?*'

The employee asks again, 'Where are your *parents*? There's a curfew for all kids under 18. You can't enter without your parents, so go home or come back with them.'

Nico and I both explode with laughter. Neither of us could believe this employee suspects us to be under 18. We both bent over laughing and Nico responds, barely able to hold his words together, 'I'm sorry, but can you say that again? It feels so good to hear I still look so young.' The employee looks at us harder in the light and apologizes. Nico kept laughing and points at me saying, 'He's 30! That *bitch* wishes he was under 18 again!'

"I'm 27." Elle says in a child-like voice while sipping her wine through the golden straw and looking right into Michelle's eyes.

"Oh yeah, I guess the wine should have been a hint, huh?" Michelle chuckles.

Becca leans forward as if to examine Elle. "I have a daughter that's about your age, her name is Brandi. She graduated from Centennial High School."

Elle twists up her face as she ponders if she knows the girl, "The name sounds very familiar, but I don't think I know her. I graduated from the Marine Oceanographic Academy."

"Oh my goodness, you were a MOA student? That's the school that's a part of Westwood High School, right? You must have been in one of the first classes." Becca excitedly points out.

"Well, *yes*, actually." Elle says proudly, although she hates the fact that MOA is associated with Westwood; the two have totally different cultures. Westwood is a typical inner-city school similar to those portrayed in movies like *Stand and Teach* or *The Freedom Writers*, whereas MOA is more like a hybrid preppy, hippy academy that stands focused on marine sciences. Most of the students would have been considered nerdy or dorky by the 80's-90's culture, but in Elle's time, they were the definition of cool.

"I was even the salutatorian." She states, repositioning herself more upright and proud. "I would have been valedictorian, *but*..." Her head drops and she lets out a massive, audible sigh. "Sam, my *rival*, managed to get just a few more hours of community service in over me which put *them* ahead. I wasn't so concerned with community service since I was getting more involved with science institutes and learning more about things that I might be able to do as an actual career, so... I let them have it." She nods as she pulls her sangria straw up to her lips and sips.

"You mean, let '*him*' have it?" Michelle asks.

"No, I meant, '*them*'. Sam was... I mean *is – they're still living* – non-binary and transitioning from male to female. No one knew until the end of the school year." Elle explains.

"*Wow*, the world you all live in today is so confusing to me. I remember when it was just *him* or *her*. It wasn't so complicated." Michelle rebuttals the terminology.

"*Girl*, I can barely keep up myself." Nico continues, "I remember when it was just 'LGBT', then we started adding in all these other letters 'QIA+' and if you talk to anyone that's any one of them and you don't *know* they get all offended. It comes down to one thing for me... Do you wanna su–"

"*Nico!*" I sharply cut him off and he immediately stops

and pulls the glass of sangria up to his mouth as Michelle bursts out laughing.

"Well – Elle, that was very admirable of you." Becca says. "I would have wanted my daughter to go there as well, but we lived too far away in PSL. I ended up sending her to Centennial High School. She liked it well enough, but not as much as her..." Becca pauses and lifts the napkin to her mouth. The color in face drains and she looks as if she's suddenly struck with nausea. Her eyes cut to Michelle, whom takes her hand, as they look at each other teary eyed.

Michelle looks at the three of us, as Becca drops her head for a moment. "Sorry guys, we've been going through a rough patch and this has been our first outing since..." she stops and looks at Becca again, "since *my son died*." The two women smile at one another with streams flowing from their eyes. We are all silent, and taking in the moment as our eyes swell with salty liquid and we are reminded of the sting of loss.

What a thing to leave out... I get it though...

Becca breaks her silence, "I'm sorry, I didn't mean to be a buzz kill by bringing it up. We wanted to kind of escape it tonight, but we also wanted to acknowledge what happened by coming to a suicide prevention event

– albeit, we didn't *know* it was an LGBTQ one. Strange place to escape it, *right*?" She pauses to gather her thoughts and attempts to share more, "He took…" her voice breaks as her bottom lip quivers, "he took…" her eyes begin to soak her cheeks again and she inhales as she wipes them clean, "his life… earlier this year."

The shock of these words spreads across the restaurant– like a blackout across a city – swift and without consequence. I hear a waiter gasp as the tragedy is heard by neighbors and passersby; we all sit, absorbing her words.

> *How unexpected.* These two friends, here tonight, seeking answers to their own loss, here with me as I lay mine to rest. As someone who has ventured close to the edge of forever, but fell back, I don't know what I can offer in the way of healing, but I know that we must reach for whatever exists, there, beyond us.

"*Why* would someone… why would *he* do that?!" she asks with pain and anger in her voice as she fiddles with the napkin to open it. Michelle places her arm around Becca to ease her mind and comfort her.

> *I have so many questions,* but now is not the time to ask. Becca and Michelle are both emotionally

distraught and perhaps the night is nearing its
end.

Nico abruptly changes the mood when he yells over to
the hot waiter, "Hey! Can we get some menus over here?
We need food!" Leave it to Nico to keep a moment
extended past its expiration. "Some good food helps to
heal a broken heart. As you can tell, I've been
heartbroken – *a lot.*" He rubs his belly.

Becca's eyes light up and laughter rumbles from our
table.

He did that – he saved the night, in the way that
only he could.

Nico is such a unique guy. The first day I met him, I
knew if he ever asked to date me we were getting
married. I just knew. He's a short, *fluffy* Mexican-
American that hates spicy food but loves to be spicy. We
met at a massive volunteer event called *Feeding America*.
The event served 800 meals to low-income and homeless
families in our community during Thanksgiving. It was
one of the many community soup kitchen type of
initiatives I was involved in back in the day.

Back then, he was a twinky 18-year-old college boy looking for love in all the wrong places. He found it in the most unlikely of places, a church sponsored event. We've been inseparable ever since.

My response to that situation would have been *completely* different. I'd have ended the night and let them deal with their pain in their own way, while he would force them to stay longer and work past it. I'm not sure one way is better than another, though I'm sure both are necessary – we *must* deal with our pain, but we also *mustn't* let it cripple us from continuing to live.

My grandmother, *the actual one*, told me something once that still sticks. It was during her final days in our home as we shared stories of life changing moments. She asked me if I knew the saying, 'what doesn't kill you only makes you stronger' and I told her yes – it was a common talking point for my great-grandparents. She continued to tell me that she didn't believe it to be true. She often thought, what if something doesn't kill you, but it breaks you and you just go on living – broken. She told me, I think most people are living life like that, just broken.

Since then, I've wondered what it was that broke her.

Aren't we though? The moment we mature from child to adult seems like it coincides with some event that breaks us apart and reconditions us.

So I wonder, are we all walking around broken and just getting worse with time as life wears down the bits that were previously left over from the last terrible event?

Will Becca and Michelle heal, or will they continue to walk this Earth more fragmented each day?

Will I?

"Finally!" Nico exclaims as the food appetizers he ordered arrive at the table. "Ladies, please – lets try a round of their appetizers and let Sid and I pay for them. I insist, partly as a thank you for bidding so high on his piece, but also to celebrate you, your strength, and your amazing presence." Nico reaches across the table and takes both their hands and raises them in celebratory joy.

No man I know honors the female spirit better.

My sister sits and smirks in response to the sight of him, but she quickly joins in by lifting her glass and offering a toast, "Cheers to good people that suffer terrible losses. May love heal you."

In unison, we shout, "Cheers!"

Becca and Michelle smile and for a moment they are comforted amongst us. Michelle mouths a *thank you* to Nico for saving the night, and I smile and place my hand on his shoulder to second it.

Staying silent and contemplative is both my strength and my character flaw simultaneously. As if my mind is calculating its response, changing with each moment's influence, and fear or anxiety.

Maybe my past experience keeps me from adding words that may be misinterpreted or rejected.

Everyone at this table has offered some form of comfort, but me. I'm just here, trapped in my own skin in this tight shirt, lost in thought and wondering *who's* son we're actually talking about.

I wonder what the relationship is here, between these two and the son. Becca's too old to have been Michelle's son's wife... but then again... My mom has dated men as young. What if... No – the sangria must finally be hitting me.

Elle brings us back to a point that Michelle made about the *high* bids. "Michelle, earlier you mentioned your shock about the high bid that the high schooler received..." Michelle nods. "So, I've gotta ask 'cause there's this 10,000 pound elephant in the room. What about Becca's bid on my brother's work? What's that about?" Elle lifts her sangria and sucks hard on the straw as if she just dropped a bomb and anxiously waits to see what everyone does.

Michelle inhales excitedly and nearly chokes on her sangria. Becca pounds away at her back with an open palm. Michelle starts to laugh as her eyes water up from the coughing. "*Whew*! Just come after me why don't you, Elle."

Before Michelle can form an answer, Becca interjects. "I don't mind telling you, hunny. We came out tonight to make a donation to the organization in the wake of what's happened to our families, and the plan was to donate smaller amounts to various artists throughout the night, but... After meeting and talking to your brother, seeing his artwork... and I don't know, something magical in the night air, Michelle and I agreed to donate everything at once for his piece."

"*Oooh*! I see. So whereas you would have donated like $500 for 20 artists, you went all in at $10,000.00 for one. Wow – *thank you*! You have no idea how long he's struggled to break through the glass ceiling that you both shattered tonight." Elle tells Becca and Michelle.

"So, did my words influence how you felt about the piece?" I follow up, but Becca quickly shuts me down.

"Now that we've gotten back on the rails again, please continue with your story." Becca asserts to me

I nod, but a part of me feels mocked for being asked to tell such a pointless story in the face of what these two women are dealing with. My words, my experience, *that* era of my life is so trivial to what they probably need to hear right now. Before, I was telling the story for the excitement of sharing a part of myself with an art buyer, but now it's more of a distraction for people suffering a great loss. That paints it in a whole different light for me. I literally have nothing to offer them – no comfort, no good distraction, and at the moment, not even a smile.

"Oh *yeah...*" I trail. "Actually, let me go use the bathroom real quick, then I'll finish telling the story." I get up from my seat and push in my chair.

"Alright, but don't run off!" Becca yells as I make my way to the restroom. It's as if she could read my mind because that's exactly what I want to do.

I enter the unisex, one person restroom and chuckle at the ongoing debate in the United States over boy's and girl's restrooms in schools. Random thoughts like that are triggered by such signs and sights. They don't do us much good, but there they are - taking up space in our heads.

I get to the urinal and think about what I'm going to tell Becca and Michelle. Perhaps I went further back in my story than I needed to. Maybe I should just tell them the boy in the picture is someone I loved that didn't love me back - it's no simpler than that. Cut out all the drama, cut out all the details, just get to the point and be done with it.

As I'm thinking, I absentmindedly shake *it* several times at the urinal as someone else enters the restroom. Another random thought crosses my mind, something I heard from a movie or someone in boy scouts, I'm not sure.

> *Shake it more than three times, and you're just playing with yourself.*

I snicker at the thought, considering that the guy who just walked in might have seen me and imagined the same thing. Misperceptions are so easily had, timing is everything.

That's true of my story too. It took time to develop the feelings that fueled what happened and lead me to the place I'm at today. Without *knowing* the background, someone's perspective of *Culture Rebel* would be skewed.

I wash my hands without any further distractions and return to the table where all the appetizers have arrived just before me. The waiter is crouched down between Becca and Michelle as I hear them exchanging some kind words and an embrace.

> *Even the waiter... has more to offer than I do. I'm ashamed as I take my seat and feel the corners of my lips turn slightly down. I don't want to tell my story that is not worth hearing. This is dumb.*

"Michelle... I..." Everyone turns to look at me. Their eyes pressure the words into hiding as I feel like either way I'm going to look like a dick. "Well, to both of you, I don't have any words to offer in comfort. In fact, each time I've lost someone the last thing I cared to hear was, 'I'm sorry for your loss.' I empathize with your pain and loss, and I wish I could have known your son to have been one more friend on his side against that dark night. Maybe it's cliche to think that one person could make a difference, and *we all* take that responsibility when someone dies – *don't we*? But you never know what impact you're having on another person – so cliche though it may be, I still wish it had been so."

Michelle and Becca smile and both mouth a *thank you* to me. Finally, I've offered something to them, but it still feels like nothing to me.

"Brother, please continue your story. Becca and Michelle are anxious to know more of the inspiration behind the art they just bought", Elle informs me. "While you were gone, *Becca* was telling us how much she loved the mood of your piece and what drew her to it." Elle jabs at the fact that she knows a little more than I do.

"It kind of... really looks like a *memory*. The way you faded the boy's face, and covered it with all that texture and even the color adds some mystery to it, ya know? Like you *lived* it." Becca added. "I have a feeling this is *the story* we all need to hear tonight."

"Listen... I'm probably giving you way more details than you really need to understand it. I was a little overzealous that someone wanted to know more about my inspiration, because it's not often that anyone asks for it in depth – but now I feel like I've spent too much of your time getting to the point. See, back in..."

Nico interrupts me and I glare at him, "*No, no.* Sid, tell

her the *whole* story. You never get to actually let it all out. Tonight's the night." Nico uses his eyes to signal to me that I should continue on as I was, so I look over to Elle and she does the same.

> *I've told this story so many times in my life* that it's like a broken record that keeps on repeating the same track. I've actually been trying to quit, it's just sad and tiring being the only one that holds onto something that someone else let go of and forgot about decades ago. Ugh, that thought alone is nauseating – decades ago.
> 'I'm so sick of that same old love...'

CHAPTER 5
TORN

"*OK*." I tell them, confirming their requests. "Actually, Elle's rival in high school reminds me of what happened back in middle school. Despite all the anxiety I suffered at the time, my grades were stellar. In most of my classes I was one of the top students, especially social studies.

One day, a new kid in social studies was pointed out by the teacher for having tied with my top score on a test. Actually, he wasn't even new, I just didn't notice him in my class before. The teacher told me in front of the class that I'm no longer the *only* top dog and with that a rival was born.

He was a white boy that was close to my height, but shorter. He had blonde hair, a trendy *bowl* haircut, a single stud diamond earring in his left ear, and clothes that reminded me of every bully I ever faced growing up. He was the embodiment of every boy I avoided at school and in each class that we shared, we were constantly compared to each other and made to be rivals.

Eventually, we bought into the idea and it became just that. Competing for right answers on questions in class, striving to achieve over each other on projects, and constantly glaring at one another from across the room. Our rivalry superseded my anxiety and before long, I was so distracted with beating him that I rarely felt the symptoms anymore."

"*Woah*, that's some serious competition." Becca responded. "The cure for your anxiety was good old fashioned rivalry... Who'd have guessed?"

"Yeah, I didn't know that that's how you overcame your anxiety." Nico adds.

"Oh, I didn't overcome it. It resurfaced years later, but I'm getting to that." I snicker. "It's all tied together."

Elle and Michelle sit back and continue listening as they dip into the appetizers. "Keep going brother," Elle demands as she plugs food into her mouth.

"*Right* – So, this boy and I... we had become great rivals and I kept my distance from him because he reminded me of everyone that ever hurt me. But as luck would have it, life put him directly in my path. One day I'm leaving the lunch line, on my way to sit with my one and only friend – Kris, but *someone else* was sitting there with him. The closer I walked, the more I realized it was him, my *rival.*

When I reached the table, my eyes immediately teared up at the feeling that I had lost my last safe harbor from the hell of middle school. I stood there at the end of the table looking at them as they both looked at me.

Kris said to me, 'look, we have a new friend!' My eyes met his and his met mine. We both glared at one another, and I internally debated what I should do, but before I could act, Kris hopped up and told me that he's running to the bathroom. Leaving me there with *him*. On his way past me, Kris told me to 'play nice'.

Naturally, that only enraged me more, but I took a seat and tried to eat my cookie. My hands shook the whole time and I could barely look at him. I felt him looking at me and it made my body just fall apart at the joints like a *crash dummy*. His gaze was heavy and hot and

I broke down beneath it. For the first time since our rivalry started, I *felt* defeated. The *embodiment* of my fears sat at my booth, seated across from me where once sat my only friend.

'Hi', he said to me. 'I'm *Gavin*'.

Then he reached out his hand for a handshake. I shot my eyes up to him and looked at him cautiously as prey would look at a predator. I thought this must be some trick; he'd pretend to be friendly then show his true colors as the bully I was sure he was. I took his hand and shook it, telling him, 'I'm Siddael'.

'I know' he told me. 'We have class together. We're *rivals*,' he joked, and giggled while his eyes softened on me.

We talked and found that we had more in common than I'd have imagined, but not in the way that most people start off. Our discussions were about behaviors of other people, philosophies, and reflections on experiences. We rarely talked about superficial subjects without going more in depth beyond what poor Kris could keep up with.

From then on, Gavin joined us every day. We talked more and more, becoming friends. Soon, Gavin was visiting my house, the first school friend to visit since Michael, and I was visiting his. We found similar *stuff* in each other's rooms.

We both had matching Teenage Mutant Ninja Turtle coin banks!

There was so much so similar between us, it was uncanny. Even our birthdays were both on the 13's of different months. We became the very best of unlikely friends, and with his presence in my life all the depression and anxiety I had just... evaporated. He was such a blessing to my wretched life when he came to be part of it.

Unfortunately, it didn't last that way for long. During that school year, the district re-zoned and changed bus routes. *Lincoln Park Academy*, our middle school, was no longer zoned for where Gavin lived, and he was going to have to switch schools. I remember when he called me after he found out and we both felt sick to our stomachs over it. My anxiety immediately returned. I couldn't imagine a day in school without Gavin."

"Somebody was a little *cray cray* for Gavin!", Nico jokes, laughing at his own words. Everyone joins him and I chuckle along with a good light punch to his shoulder. "*Ow*! Ok, I was just kidding. I had to though, it's true."

"Well – I guess to some extent I was. In fact, it was so upsetting to me that my great-grandparents contacted Gavin's parents to make them an offer. They didn't want me to be depressed like I was before, so they offered to meet his parents halfway every morning to pick him up so he could ride the bus with me to school."

Becca excitedly inhales deep and chokes on her own saliva like Michelle did earlier. She clutches Michelle's hand and we all jump up in fear that she's choking.

"Oh my goodness..." She breaths and sighs.

"*Lord* woman, you scared me!" Elle shouts at Becca.

"I'm sorry, hunny." She giggles and coughs at the same time. "It just caught me *incredibly* off-guard."

I can't help but wonder why.

"The depth to which you were loved by your great-grandparents for them to be willing to do that. Just *wow*. Then, the way that the boy impacted your life. It's very inspiring. Did he understand how you felt back then." Becca postulates.

"I don't think so, but maybe." I answered, "Boys don't exactly talk about their feelings like that and I wasn't trying to *kill* a good thing I had going. His existence in my life positively affected my health. He was like… like a part of me. Gosh that sounds weird to say, but it was like we were maybe broken in all the right places to fit together wonderfully."

"So, what happened? Did he get to keep going to school with you?" Michelle asked nervously.

"It was too late." I answered. "His parents had already switched him to Southern Oaks Middle School and Lincoln Park had a waiting list, so I guess someone else took his spot quickly. But, the beautiful thing about my friendship with him was that it transcended space and time. It didn't matter that we were separated like that, because we maintained our relationship by calling each other with updates on life every so often. At first it was days, then weeks, and eventually we would go months without talking, but the moment we did it was as if no time had passed at all. As long as I had him in my life, I was OK." Tears fill my eyes as I recollect my feelings for Gavin and relate the loss to Michelle and Becca.

"I learned an amazing lesson from Gavin about prejudices. While I was accustomed to other people treating me with such prejudgements, I didn't realize that I had some of my own towards others until I met him. I mistook him for a bully and almost missed out on the single greatest friendship I had yet discovered. He opened my eyes to the internal biases that my experiences created and I spent years trying to detangle them from who I wanted to be." I share, "That's still a work in progress, but I'm getting there one experience at a time."

"Are you and Gavin still friends?" Becca asks.

Sigh. "We haven't spoken to each other for 21 years." I answer back. "You'd think that's an easy no, but it isn't for me. I'm just that friend that he's forgotten about and that he owes a massive heartfelt apology.

After he left LPA, I was on my own again. I was befriended by many of the outcast social groups, but I found I didn't really fit in with them either. I was just present like an *innocent bystander* or a *background extra*. Another boy and I became very close, but we didn't develop the closeness that Gavin and I had.

What I was discovering is that most boys were very, very limited in the scope of what they had to talk about or do. If it wasn't about girls, sex, drugs, or games, there weren't too many other subjects they could stay on for long.

Gavin and I never touched those subjects, which I appreciated since it meant that my sexuality never came up, whether I was out or not. But, with all the other male *friends* I made, it was a constant hassle. Other boys would question the sexuality of guys that hung out with me because I was *obviously gay* since I never talked about sex with girls.

It's ironic... even though all those boys were straight, they did a *lot* of really gay things that lead me to think that homosexuality is something we're all capable of, but that would also be cliche of me to say, wouldn't it?"

"Nah, I think I agree." Michelle spurts out as Becca shoots a surprised look at her. "I think we all go through a *stage* where we question what we like, maybe experiment a little, and come to a conclusion. Some of us move past it, some of us stick to it." She states with confidence. "I had my own little moment where I thought I might be a lesbian."

"*No–*" Nico gasps as he props his head up on his hands. Elle giggles at his childlike astonishment.

"Oh *yeah*, definitely. I had this girl-friend... that's a girl who's a friend, to be clear... named Betsy that I got drunk with one night and we made out." Michelle tells us as Becca smiles and pushes her friend in the side. The push tickles Michelle and she laughs as she moves to block Becca's fingers. "Ouch, quit it!"

"Michelle, you *never* told me that!" Becca exclaims.

"Well, why would I? It never came up in conversation before. What, am I just gonna start off one night with talking about my big, fat lesbian make out session?" Michelle tosses at Becca. "Besides, hunny, I know what the church you go to is like. It's a *tad* homophobic – and that's ok, I get that. I used to be like that too." Michelle tells Becca.

"Michelle..." Becca's eyes open wide. "I am *not* homophobic."

"*O-K*. Like I said Bec, that church you go to isn't exactly *inviting* to the gays." Michelle retorts.

"I am *not* my church." Becca states as she profusely pounds her hand on her chest.

"Calm down." Michelle suggests as she places her hands on Becca's sides. "I *understand*. It's ok, I'm *telling* you I get it. I'm just also saying that being a part of that congregation made me think you must be like-minded right. I *prejudged* you.

See, I'm guilty of it too. The more we all talk, the more we understand about each other and see that we are much more alike than we think, or in some cases might like to believe."

"We're all guilty of that." Nico adds into the conversation. "Before I met Sid, I heard all kinds of shit about him from his ex-best friends. They had him painted as this terrible human being that I should never have the misfortune of knowing, but ya know what? They were just hurting from his absence in their lives. Some people find a way to blame others, whether that's an individual or a group of people, for their troubles.

When I *met* Sid, I found the most kind and giving person I had ever known. He'd take his shirt off his back for someone that needed it, but I know if the same were asked of any of the people that condemned him, they'd take it from someone else before ever giving up something of their own first."

Nico looks at me and takes my hand under the table.

Becca takes a long swig of her sangria before issuing another rebuttal, "But I'm *really* not homophobic. I just want to make that crystal clear. My husband... that's a different story."

Michelle rolls her eyes, "You mean soon to be *ex*-husband, that asshole."

Becca smacks her on the hand in response. "Yes, soon-to-be. The situation has led us to a fork in the road of our relationship. We've separated."

No one wanted to ask what happened, but we were all wondering it. It's like a car wreck in passing. You don't wish ill on anyone, but you pass by wanting to see a dead body. Whatever the reason is for wanting to, I cannot describe even to myself, but there is a yearning for the observance of death and destruction that we all have. When we learn that someone has ended something, be it their life or a relationship, we're curious as to why and what happened?

"Basically, he blamed me and that's as far into it as I want to get tonight." Becca read our minds and gave us an answer that only gave us more questions.

With no reference to what she was blamed for, I think we collectively catch it linked to *Michelle's* son's death. It's the only thing we've talked about tonight that's *heavy*.

"Right, and that makes him an asshole – 'nough said." Michelle finishes.

"Sid, what was coming out like for you? I remember you said you started dealing with it when you were 10, but when did you actually start telling people?" Becca asks.

"*Ah*, I *started* coming out when I was 13. It was a terrible time in my life because my great-grandfather had just died. I felt like he didn't really get to know me before he was gone, ya know? Like he left the world before I was unveiling this new part of myself." I share with the table.

"Oh hunny, he *knew* you. Anyone that loved you as much as he did, *knew* all the parts of you that really matter. Not for nothin', but he probably knew more about you than you even realized about yourself at the time. Parents are like that sometimes, and it burns us up when they're right. Somehow we just *know*." Michelle says as she pats Becca on the back.

"After I came out, my great-grandmother told me that he suspected I was gay. She said that when I was a baby, he'd hold me in his arms and I'd twirl his chest hair between my fingers. Something about that made him feel like I had some *sugar in my tank*." I confessed.

"*Sugar in your tank*?!" Michelle quipped. "What's *that* mean?!"

Becca cuts in, "It's an old southern way of saying *gay*." They both laugh.

"Yeah, so I guess they had their suspicions, like everyone else. My mom told me she knew since I was 6-years-old. Apparently in kindergarten I drew a picture of me and my best friend at the time getting married. She asked who I was marrying in the picture and I told her, Matthew."

I continue, "Doesn't it make you wonder, if you never told any kids the differences between genders or conditioned them to want one or the other, what would they choose on their own? When I was growing up, my great-grandparents never really stressed sexuality to me the way that I see kids done today. Not to get political, but I've witnessed many three-year-olds being asked by adults if they've gotten a boyfriend or girlfriend yet.

We are accused of having an agenda to indoctrinate kids, but... what is *that*? I don't know any gay people that go around to kids asking about their love lives... nor pressuring them to find someone, period. What I have seen and heard are demonstrations and conversations about finding what makes an individual happy and feel fulfilled with life."

Fuck you, Florida Governor Ron DeSantis and every Republican that supported the 'Don't Say Gay Bill'!

"Wow, that's a good point." Michelle says as she crosses her arms. "I can honestly say that I'm guilty of that. I never thought about it from that point of view, ya know? *Damn*, that really just blew my mind. *Shit*."

"While I was in college in California, these debates popped up all the time." Elle shares. "Once, the discussion got so heated that one of the students had to be removed from the classroom. The prof wanted students to know though that discussions like this, heated as they may become, are necessary. If we don't address the issues within our society, then we continue the ignorance that suppresses valuable contributors to our democracy.

I say *that* to say..." Elle directs her eyes and attention to Michelle, "I'm really impressed by your vulnerable acknowledgement of your own ignorance and support of that behavior prior to this conversation. I wish everyone was as open-minded as you just showed yourself to be, Michelle."

Michelle has a look on her face like a deer caught in headlights, so Nico tries to re-interpret for Elle, "What *Stanford* over there meant was that it's impressive that you didn't get offended and owned your part in making kids believe they're straight before they know the difference." Everyone bursts out laughing.

"Oh ok, *thank you*, Nico!" Michelle says as she uncrosses her arms. Her body language shows that she feels safe. I think we all do.

Maybe I can tell this story tonight after all.
Maybe here, it will be appreciated.

"I gotchu, girl! I know how it is to be around these eggheads too long." Nico laughs and glances over to see my sister and me throwing daggers with our eyes. He continues to sip his sangria pretending not to see us until he's sucking air through the straw.

"I think it's done, Nico." I tell him, annoyed by the sound.

"Yup, it's time for another pitcher! Sid, come on and catch up. You haven't finished your drink OR your story yet!" Nico jabs at me. "Sippin' ass *bitch*."

"Good things in good time, Nico." I remind him, "All good things come in good time..."

CHAPTER 6

BLEACH

"When I finally accepted the *gay* label that people had already assigned to me, I came out to some of my cousins first. One was my older, second cousin who was a displaced homemaker trying to get back up on her feet. The other was a younger cousin, who was in a bad situation with her parents. When they embraced me over the news, it was enough support to give me courage and not fear *total* rejection.

Next I told my close friends. Kristal and I had made up over her treachery in the cafeteria, so I called her and Kris – who ended up sticking around to be a friend. But, in the moment that I told them, fear got the best of me and I came out as *bisexual* instead." I share with an awkward smile.

"Now why would you do that?" Becca asks. "You're halfway there, why wouldn't you just let it out?"

"It felt easier to be *bi* than to be *gay*, because people could accept that I find men attractive as long as I *also* found women attractive. It helps them relate to the experience. If someone can relate, there is less likelihood that they'll reject it." I continue to explain, "that was the thought that ran through my head when I told them. And unfortunately, I was right. Kris's reaction was, '*Whew*, at least you're not a full blown homo.' Where Kristal sat quietly for a moment while I panicked, but she eventually told me that she suspected since the whole Michael crisis. It wasn't the welcoming I had hoped for, but it wasn't exactly rejection either.

I decided to tell another close male friend of mine, but he already knew. He and I had some *shared* experiences that probably helped him define his sexuality, but I also think it led to some terrible confusion for him." I look at everyone's eyes to see the questions forming just behind them, "Don't get me wrong, I'm not trying to be cryptic, I've just never said any of this out loud before. I've never told *anyone* about Ryan."

Elle's face immediately puzzles up as she's hit by realization. She gasps and pushes her hand into her chest as her body falls back into her seat as though she's been deeply offended, "Excuse me?! *Ryan*?! The *best friend* I remember?! What now?!" she exclaims to me as all eyes fall upon her.

"I *knew* there was something up with you two!" she says as she points an accusatory finger at me and leans forward adjusting her comfort in the chair. She's primed for the story to continue to fill in the gaps that she's wondered about all these years.

Mmhhm. "Yes – keep going, I'm very curious about how this played out," Becca murmurs. Michelle stays seated back as she chews on some ice cubes from the sangria and Nico continues to pick at the remainder of the appetizers.

"Well, after Gavin left and I was a floater between outcast groups, I got very close to a boy named Ryan. He had a pale white complexion with freckles, and he was a little taller than me; a brunette with the *then-still popular* bowl haircut. I don't remember how our friendship really got started, or what drew us to be as close as we became, but he held on tight to our friendship and I held onto his.

Our friendship was *different* from me and Gavin's because Ryan was our opposite. He was loud, he used curse words for every other word in a sentence, he had a terrible anger issue, he loved to constantly make someone else the butt-end of a joke, he was a little dumb – though I'd never *tell* him that, and he talked about girls in the absolutely most deplorable way. He was what I believed and feared Gavin was, yet I accepted Ryan thanks to Gavin's intervention in my life.

Ryan knew I was gay, but he defended me to the point of fighting when anyone questioned my sexuality, meanwhile, an extraordinary amount of sexual tension existed between us. We explored it in the most innocent of ways, like when we were alone we'd lay in a bed with each other and spoon or we'd share soft, careful touches when no one was looking. I'd move his hair out of his face and run my fingers along the side of his face down to his chin. He'd smile at me with the kindest of eyes and hug me so tight that I'd..." I pause as I realize something for the first time, myself.

Ryan loved me?

"Well, you get the idea. Ryan *knew*." I state to the table.

"So, wait. Was *he* gay too?" Michelle barks, "I don't get it, why would you two have sexual tension if he wasn't?"

"To be honest, straight men aren't as *straight* as you think they are, Michelle." Nico chuckles as he fingers cheese off his face left there from a cheese covered tortilla chip. He licks his fingers, and continues. "Most of the dicks I sucked were attached to a *straight* guy."

Michelle's mouth drops open. "*Wooow*. Just wow." Michelle says in response.

"I've talked about this with my male friends before because some of them are *very* questionable." Elle adds to the conversation. "These days they do all that, spoon, kiss each other on the cheek. It's much more open and generally accepted, but it sounds to me like there was a little more going on there with Ryan – whom I did *not* know this about."

"It didn't seem so *romantic* at the time. Honestly, I never questioned Ryan's sexuality until right now. I just accepted each moment as they came. Thinking back, just before I came out, Ryan and I spent a night together that pushed the boundaries of our friendship and *probably* his sexuality.

He visited my great-aunt's oceanfront place one weekend in Micco, where I took him out on a wave-runner to meet my fishing buddy, Miguel – who was also straight, but gave me my first kiss." Everyone's eyes light up to the comment. "That's a whole story to itself."

"Unfreakin' believable." Michelle comments and swats Becca on the arm, "I can't believe how many straight boys are so *gay*." she chuckles again.

"Right?! Me neither, but thank God for 'em." Nico spurts.

"Well, my memory of that weekend is hazy, but I remember the following morning. We laid in bed together and the sexual tension between us reached a climax. My hands ran up and down his body as our lips crossed over each other's over and over again – just barely kissing. A nagging thought crossed my mind during the experience that stopped me from exploring further. I didn't know what Ryan really *thought* about *us*, but I was sure he wasn't going to become my boyfriend and while I loved Ryan as the amazing friend he was, I wasn't *ok* with *just* being friends with benefits either.

> A few years later, absolutely – I would have explored his body and not thought twice. In my 20s, I was a hoe all day and all night. But I was fragile when I knew Ryan."

Nico raises his hand, "Been there and done that! Hashtag growing up gay!"

"Exactly. Most young gay boys are the sexual experiment for straight boys; maybe it would be more accurate to say that boys have sex with each other and those that develop emotional connections stay gay. The others move on and *probably* end up bi-sexual or straight. For those of us that *stay* gay, we feel like we're discarded or rejected by our friend-lovers at some point when we no longer meet their needs or fit their lifestyle. We're treated as a stain on their character rather than celebrated as a part of their individual identity's development.

I don't know that Ryan would have treated me like *that*, or if I had continued with that experience that it would have changed the outcome of his sexuality, but I didn't want to risk the loss of his friendship. So that was the last time we came close to crossing that boundary.

In fact, it was the last time we enjoyed each other's company at all. Following that weekend, he began dating a girl that didn't like my existence in his life and she drove a wedge between us. When I came out as bisexual, Ryan surprised me by throwing a temper tantrum. I remember his remarks to me were that he 'defended' me and that he couldn't believe that I ended up being gay anyway.

His girlfriend assumed that I was trying to *steal* him away, and his anger towards me became hate. He betrayed our friendship, rejected me, and began to tell people that I was trying to 'turn him gay.'"

"Maybe all that sexual tension between you...caused him to have conflict within himself?" Becca offers. "Woah, I just realized we're talking about teenagers, here. That's crazy to me – you guys were just babies!"

"I don't know, Bec. Speaking for myself, we did some pretty crazy stuff when we were teens too." Michelle scoffs and Becca turns to deviously smile at Michelle.

"*Still...*" Becca claims.

I continue, "Society would like to make it seem like teenagers are *too young*, but nature dictates otherwise, doesn't it? Puberty happens whether someone is ready or not, and hormones change everything. Actually, I have a whole theory about that thanks to my observations of Ryan, but that's for another conversation.

After I was rejected by most of the outcast groups, Kristal left *Lincoln Park Academy* to go to *Fort Pierce Central*, following some bullying that she faced and Kris no longer wanted to associate with me because people thought that he was gay... *because of me.*"

I giggle at the thought. "But despite all those setbacks... I was OK. *Why*?"

"Because you..." Elle starts to answer and I join in to speak it in unison, "*still* had Gavin."

"Yes, while all this was happening and I was losing the few friends I had, I *still* had Gavin in my life." I tell the table.

"I don't remember you mentioning how you came out to him and how he took it. Did you?" Becca asks.

"Yes." I reply to Becca, "It went like this. I called him up one day and told him I had something important to tell him that might change our friendship, but I needed to say it. 'I'm gay.'"

"So to *Gavin*, you tell him you're gay and *not* bisexual?" Becca asks.

I feel a little embarrassed, but I explain further, "Yeah – so being bisexual lasted a whole week for me. After I came out as bi and the news quickly spread, a girl approached me that also identified as bi and wanted to date me. Honestly, if I was going to go with a girl, she'd have been it. She was a fighter, kind of mean, absolutely gorgeous, but not in the conventional way of being pretty in makeup while wearing sexy clothes, more in the way of her strong features, attitude and how she reminded me of my mom."

Everyone laughs at the thought.

I continue, "I felt no romantic or emotional pull toward her. In fact, there were no girls that ever solicited those feelings from me. Following that I stopped being bi and told everyone I'm *just* gay. I was losing friends for being bi, so then what did I have to fear anymore?"

Ugh! "I can't stand when a man pretends to be into a girl and keeps leading her on, just to keep up appearances or for entertainment or whatever his self-serving reason is. I always felt it was noble that you didn't do that to a girl, brother." Elle shares, shaking her head side-to-side in discord with the idea.

"Second that!" Michelle agrees.

"*Thank you*! I don't see a point in lying to anyone about it. Heartbreak *sucks*." I relate to my sister and Michelle. "When I told Gavin, there was no hesitation in his response. He quickly fired back with, 'is that it?'

I was trembling on the phone with fear, but he continued to tell me, 'It doesn't matter to me if you're gay or straight. I love you just the same. You're like a brother to me.' That was the first time Gavin told me he loved me, and from then on we'd tell each other 'I love you' when we hung up.

The shabby world that grew around me in his absence was literally falling apart, and I was more and more alone. But I still had Gavin; so I could endure any of this. Within the year, I found another outcast group to belong to, and began my journey towards reconstruction in the social hierarchy of school.

Then... a *new* tragedy struck that I was completely unprepared for; my great-grandfather died."

Tears swell in my eyes, compelling me to take a swig of the watery sangria in my glass. Reliving the moment takes a toll on my emotional state. Years separate us from the trauma of loss, *but whether a day or 10,000*, it still feels like yesterday to the heart. Everyone at the table empathizes with my loss and tears start flowing all around. The waiter passes by and brings both a bill and *another* pitcher of sangria to our table.

"I know you guys didn't order it, but I've been hearing some of your conversation here and there, and... I just think you all could use this, so... it's on the house." The waiter tells us.

"Oh my God, thank you, hunny!" Michelle yelps as she pours a glass.

"Thank you so much sweetie, that was very kind of you. Please tell your manager thank you for us." Becca adds.

"You know you gonna get that good tip! You see all these tears over here and bring more alcohol!" Nico squints, "You gettin' that *good*, good tip."

Elle laughs at Nico and thanks the waiter as I nod my head in thanks to him.

Everyone throws their cards into a pile for the check to be split equally as they wipe the tears from their eyes and fill their cups. The waiter and another employee of the restaurant come to clear away plates and empty glasses, leaving us with the pitcher and time to finish the story.

"*Alriiight.*" Michelle says. "Let's get on with the tearjerker."

Everyone giggled, but there's probably some truth to that sentiment of not wanting to be moved to such an emotional place, especially for whatever loss they've had. I try to keep that in mind, though loss is at the core of *Culture Rebel*.

I nod in agreement. "My great-grandfather had fallen ill around the time that I started having anxiety in the 6th grade. His illnesses and their treatments began to complicate each other. An ulcer affected his heart, his heart medication affected his ulcer. He had multiple surgeries for his heart, some of which resulted in a severe staph infection that required skin grafts from his thighs. Ultimately, though he was diagnosed with and died from Leukemia and all the complications it created with his other illnesses.

> It was the first time my family was without their patriarch, the first time my great-grandmother was without her husband, and the first time I was without a father. I still had my *biological* father, but he didn't raise me and I didn't live with him.

> *This* man – he was my father. Seeing him there, lifeless, with my great-grandmother sobbing at his feet, asking him not to leave her was the greatest loss and deepest pain I had known at that point in

my life. It took me to a new low. Hell, it took all of us to a new low. On top of it, my mom was sentenced to 1-year in prison for a violation of probation."

"What'd she do?" Michelle inquires.

"She admitted to smoking a joint." Elle responds. "That's it, *one* joint. They didn't even drug test her, she told her probation officer who was a *real* bitch and she reported it to have her sent back for 1-year. Something that's now legal, she lost a *year* of her life over."

"Because of it, Elle had to come live with us." I interject. "It was rough at first, I had become used to being an only child, but it wasn't uncommon that people were randomly staying with us because of bad situations. By this time, those two cousins I mentioned earlier were gone, so now it was Elle's turn.

Our great-grandmother, Emmy, was in a terrible state of being, but Elle's presence at the house helped to keep her grounded; the responsibility of having a child gave her purpose and meaning when she needed it most."

Elle sniffles and draws my attention to her as she wipes the tears from her cheeks and adds in her experience. "I didn't know *Johnny* that well – I was only 7, but *Emmy* made it feel like home for me." Michelle reaches out and clutches Elle's hand tightly. Michelle gives her a supportive, reaffirming smile. The kind that only a mother could give, it warms you right up when you're in a cold place. I wish I had that ability within me; to make people feel warm, safe, and secure.

What a true gift that is.

I release a deep breathe of air as if I forgot to breathe and continue, "In the months that followed his death, my family tried to resume some kind of *normalcy* like going out on the boat and fishing, but that was a fantasy. Instead, new norms developed like instead of camping we stayed at my great-aunt Sandy's waterfront place.

Since I had a learner's permit, I was now the designated driver while Emmy enjoyed drinking all day and night." I chuckle, but realizing that I just revealed that the alcoholism was overtaking her. My mouth straightens and my eyelids drop with my eyes to the table. I admit, "She struggled with alcoholism as a means to deal with her pain. It wasn't *too* bad while Elle was there, but a year later, it became a real monster that we lived with..."

Nico puts his hand on my back to draw me back and I

continue, " – but that's not *today's* story. It was during one of these new normal outings that I found myself coming out to the family, unexpectedly. I told my friends and *some* family members that I was gay when I was 13, but I was 15 now and hadn't yet told my great-grandmother or her daughters who were like older sisters to me. By then, I had found and befriended other gay guys online thanks to AOL chat rooms."

"Good ol' America Online, *yesss*!" Nico shouts with a snicker in his voice.

"At 15, you were finding gay men in chat rooms?" Becca asks with a sort of accusatory tone.

"Where there's a will, there's a way, girl." Nico comments, "I was on there when I was 12. Where else could you get dick pics for free, we didn't have smartphones yet" He snickers.

"I just can't believe... at 15?" Becca continues.

"Becca, I remember my nephew stole *magazines* when he was 10 from his dad's drawer. Different times, different methods, same shit." Michelle adds.

"I wasn't looking for *dick pics* like Nico, I was looking for friends and I found them. One in particular was a 19-year-old boy in Orlando that was absolutely stunning – I know that 'cause he sent me pics of his face, *not his junk*. In fact, he was so stunning that he was going to be in a male beauty pageant, which was pretty unheard of in 2001; *here* anyway."

"Can't say I've heard of one either." Michelle calls out.

"A teenage boy beauty pageant?" Nico questions. "He was probably just trying out to be a GoGo dancer at the local gay bar, let's be real." Everyone laughs but I toss him a sarcastic glare.

"No – it was the real deal, and he invited me to come and watch it. I wanted to go there so badly and be around other gay people and meet him in person, but... *Orlando*?" I ask rhetorically.

> "That's not somewhere I could get on my own, and I didn't think that anyone would take me, but as it so happened on one of those new normal days out in the boat, Emmy, her daughter, Beth, and son-in-law, Jerry, were planning things to do and places to go that they hadn't been able to in a while and asked me if there was anything I'd like to have considered. I instantly replied, '*Orlando*'.
>
> They thought I wanted to go to a theme park, so they asked me which park, but I told them it wasn't

for a theme park, it was for... a beauty pageant.
They laughed and thought I was joking, but when
they saw my face, they cut it out and asked me
more. I explained that I knew someone in the
pageant that invited me to see *him*.

Their faces all looked puzzled, and my Jerry asked,
'You sure you don't mean a *her*, son? I ain' never
heard of a beauty pageant for men.' I shook my
head side-to-side as the realization hit me as to
where the conversation was headed. They
snickered at the idea of a *men's* beauty pageant.

Jerry asked, half-jokingly, 'Son, you got a little *sugar in your tank*?'

At that point, my lip was already quivering and my
eyes were filled with water, but – that *question*... all I could
manage was an affirming nod; then I cried out of fear,
anger, and loss. They all huddled around me and hugged
me until I stopped sobbing.

Jerry looked at me and told me that he was only
joking and didn't mean anything nasty by it. The
subsequent conversation led to an offer from Beth
to take me to a PFLAG meeting, so we could all
learn more about *being gay*."

Everyone at the table wipes their eyes again.

"*Damn it*, Sid, we don't have enough napkins for this shit!" Michelle gripes.

"To have had the challenges and struggles that you had, you were equally blessed with love and acceptance from the people that knew you best. We don't all get that in life; you really lucked out." Becca offers.

"I'm still amazed that Aunt B's first reaction was to take you to PFLAG. I really expected a Christian rehabilitation center." Elle cuts in. "Our family was so racist, homophobic, and Christian-centric that there wasn't really room for anyone to be *different*.

> Our grandma changed that when she had our mom, the *first* mixed kid in the family; She's half American and half Colombian. Then our mom kicked it up a notch by ushering in the next generation of mixed kids being half black and half white, the first of which also happened to be gay.

> With each major introduction of diversity, our family has surprised us by adapting, accepting, and embracing those differences that were once foreign and taboo.

It's really rather incredible, ya know?

Coming in on the back end of all that, I've reaped all the benefits that my mom and brother paid for in trauma." She snickers and the group giggles.

"He had fear and fretted over coming out, whereas now I think they expect all of us, especially me, to be gay or bi or something out of the ordinary." she further adds. "Surprisingly though, nope – *still* just him."

"Alright, let me recap and make sure I understand all this right." Becca says as she holds her hand up to list off points of my story on her fingers. "You weren't well-adjusted when entering middle school and experienced illness as a result of stress." Her thumb extends.

"Yep." I answer.

"All but one friend by happenstance abandoned you, then *he* introduced you to your rival who ended up your best friend." She puts up a second finger.

"That's right", I reply.

"Your best friend switches schools, leaving you alone, but you build a new social circle..." Another finger goes up.

Uh huh.

"...which includes a boundary pushing relationship with a new best friend, all of which you lose when you come out of the closet as bi-sexual." She adds to another finger.

I giggle at how strange it sounds to have my life experiences diluted down to a simple list and answer her with a head nod.

"Your great-grandfather dies, leaving you and your great-grandmother in a vacuum of grief that is partly filled with the presence of your sister..." She extends her pinky finger and her eyes widen as she realizes she'll have to use her other hand now.

"Yesss." I continue confirming for her.

"...and in the wake of his death you come out of the closet accidentally to your family." Her thumb extends on her other hand.

"Yes... that about sums it up." I answer again.

"All of that, within 3 years." She looks at me then pans the table for the look in everyone's eyes. "That's *insane*." She plops backwards against her chair back. "It should be a book. You *should* write a book. What you lived in that short span of middle school, some people don't experience in a lifetime."

Hhaha. "We say that all the time – it should be a book! But *honestly*, who's gonna read it? I can't believe you've stuck around this long to hear my story. That's rare. No one ever lets me talk this long or holds interest in what my life is like." I retort. "I don't think anyone would buy my book."

"I think not only would they buy it, they'd appreciate the insight you've provided as an alternative point of view. We need different and fresh perspectives in the world to tackle problems like racism and homophobia. Your story is bizarre and interesting – you *must* share it." She leans forward and demands with confidence.

"I'll *think* about it." I nonchalantly respond.

> *Yes the idea of telling my story in some way or another has crossed my mind,* but I really don't believe anyone would care. If people don't listen when I tell it, why would they read it or watch it?
> How many people in America want stories about the life of a gay, mixed kid?
> If they were in demand, we'd have them by now, wouldn't we?

"And... it's not done yet. Can I assume that the boy in the painting is *Ryan*? Since he was your first *physically* close friend?" She pleasantly guides me back to the reason we're gathered here tonight.

Before I can answer, the waiter returns to the table with our cards and we each take our respective receipt slips to sign our names.

As we're signing, I answer Becca. "Ladies, I know it's getting late and this place will be closing soon. Would you like to call it a night or would you like to take this conversation on a walk?"

"Oh, you're definitely not getting out of this. We've talked too long to not finish the story." Becca tells me as she stands up and looks down at Michelle as if to redirect her words, "We're walking."

Michelle's head jerkily swivels to each of us at the table as she timidly agrees, "I *guess* we're walkin'."

CHAPTER 7
DARK NECESSITIES

We exit through the glass doors of *Pickled*, huddled together and giggling like a group of teenagers. Nico and Elle wave passionately at the waiter as Michelle blows him a kiss goodnight. The evenings mixture of wine, cocktails, cider, sangria, good food and enthralling conversation has broken down the walls between us.

There are only a few people walking out on the street now, but masses of them are perched in front of the bars that line the street. When the restaurants close, people shuffle to the bars and breweries until morning. In the distance, we hear people yelling their stories to each other over an eclectic mix of loud music. Friends are gossiping, laughing, and holding onto long past memories as live bands play. Sound to keep their silent truths filled with tunes that contain lyrical truth for *someone* sitting there in the crowd with them.

The street lights provide an ambient background against the kaleidoscope of colorful lights that blast from each bar and paint the buildings around them. Each window appears as if a cutout in the fabric of reality, letting us view alternate dimensions of the human experience. Each scene, a clip out of someone's life. Most of them look fun and loud, filled with sensation, but some are private and lonely, filled with needs yet to be met.

A chill runs up my spine and down my arms lifting every hair follicle up along its veiny path. I catch the sight of us in the reflection of a window as we walk by. I wonder...

> *From the outside looking in, which clip of our*
> *conversation would I have caught?*
> *The moments that we laughed?*
> *The moments that we cried?*

In just a glance, from one second to another, a scene changes. A tear shed in a moment of loss may stream on a cheek filled by a moment of joy. We are as complicated and complex as the lights that layer those walls or the musical tones that fill the air in this beautiful night of layered loves and losses.

What a beautiful night for heartbreak.

So many *nuances* that subtly influence us; All the *things* we leave out of our stories that mattered, but are sacrificed because they don't fit neatly in a story that has an expiration. Only God will ever know the trillions of tiny happenings that lead us each to the threshold of where we stand, sit... or *lay*, tonight.

Even if I never finish telling my story, it's gratifying that I was *finally* given the moment to release some of the *incredible* weight that these details have pressed down upon me. Tonight is a testament of how our light and one's inherent shadow affects the portrait of another.

Tonight, I am freed.

We make our way to the river front and decide to walk along the sidewalk over the bridge, and come back before we call it a night.

"It's just as well, I've been slacking on my steps." Michelle comments as she preps her fitness watch for the trek.

"Me *too*. I was just in a competition for it, but all my steps were from my desk to the fridge." Nico then sets his fitness watch alongside Michelle.

"Alright, Sid. Let's have it. It's time for your crescendo." Becca states to me.

We begin our walk and with it, the end to my story.

"After I came out of the closet to my family, things only got worse for me that year." I share it with the group.

"That *surprises* me, I'd have thought things would get easier once that weight was off your shoulders." Becca says.

"I thought so too, but now I was just alone, *and* I was the token gay kid..." I pause and consider the past. "Ya know what, I can't really say I was alone – there were a few friends, but we weren't as close as I was with Gavin or Ryan; so I *felt* alone. I think it's like that for a lot of people.

There's almost always *someone* that cares about you, but you kind of take them for granted because they aren't vibing with you in a way that you need to feel connected at that moment in your life." I reply and Becca nods in agreement.

"By then I was in 8th grade and a new boy showed up at our school that gave me hope. He immediately caught my attention, not just because I found him super attractive or because he was one of the tallest guys in the school, but because I thought I met someone else in school that *might* be gay."

"How did you know?" Becca asks.

"He had a lot of *obviously* gay traits, kinda like Kris did." I answer, "Basically *stereotypes*. We all hate them, but they do tend to help us navigate some tricky situations sometimes. Case in point, I had this boy pegged as gay because he had *somewhat* effeminate mannerisms, blonde tipped spiky hair, eyebrows that were snatched before that was even a thing, he wore lots of flowery, button up 90s Hawaiian shirts – *very* gay – and tight jeans, I mean... he just had to be at *least* open minded to it." I explain to Becca.

Haha. "*Oh*, Kurt..." Elle chuckles out loud when she realizes who it was from our past. She knows Kurt thanks to being friends with his younger brother. She had met him, observed him, known him, and agreed with my assessment. He was kind to her, but treated me as a mortal enemy.

"He *hated* me because I handed him a note one day seeking his friendship. I wasn't courageous enough to talk to him directly, so I wrote what I wanted to say and nervously gave it to him. The next day I approached him and asked if he read my note, but his reaction was totally unexpected; he literally turned his nose up to me. 'Yes!' He answered me with a look of disgust on his face. When I asked him how he felt about it, he ignored me and continued to ignore me until I walked away.

Worse still, he started spreading rumors that I was gay, even though I was already out to everyone that knew me... A part of me thought he must be my *karma* for Michael, but, that *too*, is a story for another day. I say *all this* to point out that at that time in my life I was stuck in a pit and had no bonds strong enough to help me out of it. Not *yet* anyway.

That was my life 'til March, when my mom was released from prison. She stayed with Emmy and I for a while until she got back on her feet. This time, she returned as a *different* person. She was more *motherly* to me. She had more patience and spoke with kindness, not the usual quick to anger, always frustrated mom that I was used to.

She wanted to repair our relationship and began acknowledging her part in my challenges. She attempted to help me work through them by taking me on long rides to listen to music like we did when I was a toddler. The music, though, wasn't within my preferences. She thought songs from *Linkin Park* and *Metallica* would resonate with me, but I wasn't ready. She'd explain how the lyrics and tunes could help me to express my feelings, and I wrote that off as *pothead* logic.

Regardless, her renewed presence with her new mindset in my life tremendously helped to balance the scales. However, it strained my relationship with Emmy... again, another story for *another* day.

During a conversation on one of those drives we were talking about happiness when I realized the impact Gavin had on my life. She suggested that I reconnect with him since it had been nearly a year since we last spoke to each other; More than that since I actually hung out with him.

We lost touch as people often do, but in that time

Gavin had become a sort of charm for me. The thought of him was reassuring and helped me through tough times. In his absence, I became convinced that people change and cut out anyone that doesn't fit in with their new identity.

What if he had changed? What if I didn't fit into his world anymore? "

We arrived at the base of the bridge where we'll be ascending up its steep side. Elle and Nico start to climb, while Becca and Michelle pause to watch a father take a fishing pole from his son to free the line from a rock where the boy had cast it. The boy watches him with the tiniest hint of concern in his eyes, like an apology to his father, but also disappointment for not being allowed to learn from his own mistake. Just next to them, in a blue bucket, a fish flops as it gasps for air.

> *Parents always rush in to take over,* but don't they know that if we aren't given the space to figure it out ourselves, we may forever just wait for someone else to do it for us?

We continue our journey, moving up the side wall to reach the sidewalk with little more than a concrete barricade to protect us from the racing traffic on the bridge. The sea air smacks us in the face with a salty, open palm. Sprinkled in it is the scent of seaweed afloat on the water, fish in the buckets below us, and a tinge of the tasty food that was not too long ago being prepared in the restaurants from which we came. The street lights flicker above us like lantern lights with dying batteries. The fishermen below whip their lines from back to front, casting little red and white bobbers into a beautiful scene for the ending of a beautiful story.

My hands shoot up into the sky, to clap together as I quote *Sophia* from *The Golden Girls* who reminds me of Emmy, "*Picture it*! Fort Pierce 2002..." My hands move from being together to wide apart as I frame our shared sight of the city from the bridge.. Everyone giggles.

Who doesn't love the Golden Girls?

I continue...

APRIL 2002

Brrring. Brrring.

My heart races with each ring. I pace around on the

outside back porch feeling nauseous. It's been more than a year since I've seen him.

He's not going to want to hang with me.
He has a completely different life by now.

Brrring. Brrring.

I should just hang up. Yeah, I should...

"Hello?" an unrecognizable voice answers the phone.

Did I dial the right number?

"Hi?" My voice cracks. "I'm looking for... *Gavin*?" I ask. My palms are sweaty. I hate being on a phone anymore. Too many times I've been cursed out or shut down by people that were once my friends. Gavin isn't *like* that, but then again it's been a while since we've talked.

"Yeah, that's me. Who's this?" he asks, setting off panic within me.

Who's this?! Who are you? You don't sound like Gavin.

"It's Sid." I respond.

"Oh hey! What's up?! I was wondering what you've been up to." he tells me.

Whew, I'm relieved to hear that.

"Not much, *really*. I just wanted to call you and see if you wanted to maybe hangout one weekend... soon,"I explain.

"Yeah, I'd *love* to!" he tells me with excitement.

"*Really*?" I ask. I cower in fear that I'm imagining this moment.

"Yeah! When do you wanna hang?" he asks.

"Well, I know your birthday is coming up and you're probably busy that weekend, so maybe the weekend after?" I offer.

"Actually I'll be out of town that weekend, but hold up." he tells me as he muffles the phone mic with his hand before I can respond. I hear him faintly yell, "Mom!" and it sounds like he's checking with her about the dates.

"Hey, how about my birthday weekend?" he asks when he returns.

"Your *birthday*? *That* Saturday? Aren't you going to be doing something with your family or having a party?" I assert. "I don't want to take you away from your plans."

"No, no, it's cool. We're not doing anything, and I'd rather be *with you* anyway." he casually tells me..

"Alright!" I blurt. "We'll pick you up that Friday after school?"

"Let me check with my mom..." He muffles the phone again and returns within seconds. "Ok, Yeah! You still have my address?"

"Yeah, *of course*!" I reply.

"Cool, its a date then! Love you, see you then!" he tells me.

"Love you too... bye." I say back to him as I let the phone fall from my ear and press the *End Call* button. I lean my shoulder against the glass sliding door, then turn my back to it and slide down to the floor.

I'm excited... and terrified at how smooth that went and... *I guess* how excited he was about hanging out with me. Gavin doesn't really know how terrible my life has gotten; that I'm the 8th grade pariah at LPA.

When he sees me again, he'll probably see what they all see ...and reject me. But, he sounded so excited...

He said he'd 'rather be with me,' when a few seconds earlier he didn't even realize who I was by the sound of my voice.

Is this a set up? 'Cause it feels like one.

The glass sliding door starts to open; it's my mom.

"So, how'd it go?" she asks me. I stand up and move away from the door.

"*Good*, he's actually able to come on his birthday." I answer.

"His *birthday*?!" she asks with equal curiosity. "He isn't having a party or *something*?"

"Nope, he said he'd *'rather be with me'*." My eyes get glossy and she moves to hug me, picking me up and shaking me.

"See! I told you! Just trust ya momma, boy!" she squeezes me tight.

"Ok, ok! Yes. You were right, *for once*."

"Give me his number, I'm going to talk to his mom and get the details." she commands. I hand her my note and as she dials the number, I walk to my room. I have so many mixed feelings right now, but none stronger than the fear of what it'll be like the moment I see him after so long.

My mom talks to his and tells her that we're going to my great-aunt Sandy's waterfront place. There we'll be entertained with riding a wave-runner, fishing, swimming in the pool, hiking in the parks, and practically have the house to ourselves. She pretty much sold the weekend experience to her, even though it was already a done deal. I could hear Gavin's mom on the phone from my window say she was jealous of the all expenses mini-vacation her son was getting.

My little sister was staying that weekend with one of her elementary school teachers, so mom planned to drive Emmy, Gavin and I up to the house. Her boyfriend would pick her up there, then bring her back to our house in Fort Pierce, while Emmy hung out with Beth and Jerry in the guest house, leaving the main household to Gavin and I, *alone*.

Sandy's house is the ideal getaway spot, it has it all. The front gate was a huge metal one that automatically opened when a vehicle approached it. The circular driveway was cobblestone and featured one of her mosaics, a dolphin fountain center piece.

The house had huge bay windows in the front and back with amazing views that overlooked a pool and hot tub, and beyond that, the river that fed into the much larger, Indian River Lagoon.

The house has a big, open kitchen that *begs* to be cooked in, a 60" projection TV in the living room and one of those stereo systems that have tower speakers as tall as most people. All of that opened up to a grand master suite with massive wooden double doors the size of a Cathedral's. The master suite was nearly half the size of the house with a bathroom that was the size of a small apartment.

It was definitely a place he'd never forget. And it was going to be just me and him, enjoying each other's company for hours on end... in all of that.

He's going to be so bored...
How can I keep him entertained? I haven't had a friend in so long I don't know how to actually interact with anyone.

I immediately began brainstorming activities to keep us busy the entire weekend. It's going to be his birthday weekend and he's turning 15 – kind of a big deal! ...Annnd he chose to spend it with *me*. That's... HUGE.

I need this weekend to be amazing for him.

I plot out everything from our arrival on Friday afternoon to his departure on Saturday evening. Emmy observed me writing down an itinerary at the kitchen table prompting her to inquire.

"Whatcha doin' hun?" she asks from over my shoulder.

I jump up a bit out of my seat having been startled by her. She giggles at the sight. She's very good at sneaking up on me, and does it often.

"Just trying to plan Gavin's visit, writing down when we should do what so that he has a good time." I show her my plans.

"Hunny, you don't have to do all that. He can't *not* have fun." she says.

"It's his *birthday*." I remind her.

"He's been a good friend for a long time, he'll enjoy just being with you hunny." she retorts.

"I gotta make sure." I tell her as I return to looking at my paper. She puts her hand on my shoulder, and pats it a few times.

"Oh, ok. Well do what you gotta do hunny." she tells me.

The days that separated us flew by, and before I felt ready, Friday, April 12th was here. The slush of emotions I feel unsettles and excites me, equally. The school day passes by with me ignoring everyone's usual bullshit. The bus ride after school feels extra long, and I hurry home from the bus stop, moving swiftly with greater purpose.

I prance directly to my room, strip down to my underwear and get ready by bolting back and forth between there and the bathroom, performing a full body detail. I shower, wash my hair, scrub my body down with a washcloth, brush my teeth, gargle and rinse with mouthwash, then scrub my face with a special face wash that I rarely use, brush my hair, and finally layer myself in lotion, coat my armpits with deodorant, and spritz myself with some cologne.

Eventually I get around to packing and select an outfit for our *reunion*. A pile of shirts accumulate until I find the perfect one – a white *Hollister* t-shirt with the outline of a forest filling in the front body of it. I love that it contrasts my skin complexion and brightens up my face. It's one of my favorite, most expensive shirts that I rarely wear because I never have a reason to. *That*, and we have well-water that destroys white clothes. I spritz cologne on it, just to make sure the scent sticks.

I pull the shirt over my head and realize I have to brush my hair again to make sure I look *presentable*. I look in the mirror and see a foreign sight; I'm *smiling*.

A shiver runs up my spine causing my body to shake it off like a dog shakes off water after a bath. It almost feels like I'm going on a *real* date. The thought angers me.

No. Don't think that. Never think that! This is Gavin!

I wasn't attracted to Gavin when I first met him. I acknowledged he was *alright lookin'*, but that was the extent of it. Gavin's voice was more attractive than anything else to me. It was energetic and assertive with a slightly high pitch that was countered by an unexpected and intense hoarseness that has the most indescribable and unique quality I have ever known. I love it. I love to hear him talk.

I find myself deeply divided. Half of me is *offended* by the half that takes his words further than he meant them. Why'd he have said he'd *rather be with me* and that it was a date. Those words were innocent, his intent was innocent, so why am I so *apprehensive* about it?

> *Because I'm... gay? Is this just a guy thing?*
> *Like, is this how straight guys are about everything a girl says?*
> *Reinterpreting their meaning?*

I push the feelings and thoughts to stop them from tainting this weekend.

My mom and great-grandmother are preparing for the weekend in the kitchen. Both of them are working together to make cold-cut sandwiches for us to eat as snacks between meals. Some coolers and bags are sitting by the door, an indication that I'm to take them to the van. I grab my bag, then load up everything else. I run back to my room to get my CD binder and the weekend's itinerary.

Since we last hung out, my music library has expanded and I wanted to share with him some of the new songs that I listen to. My mom beacons me over as I walk through the kitchen.

"Look at this," she shows me a birthday cake in the fridge. "Emmy got it for you to give to Gavin tomorrow." My mouth drops open. My great-grandmother does many good things for many people, but buying cakes for birthdays is usually not one of them. She says it's a *job for the parents*, at least in the case of my cousins. She bought *him* a birthday cake. In many ways, it was like her way of saying *I love you*.

Gavin is so loved.

"Thank you for getting him a cake, Emmy." I express to her.

"Oh hunny, ain' nothin'." she fires back. "I just hope you both have a good time this weekend."

I pull out my itinerary and look at her with a big smile, "It's all part of the plan, Emmy!"

She giggles and replies, *"Oh-kay"*.

My mom grabs and jingles the van keys to signal to me that we have to get moving, Gavin lives way out south of us and traffic will be heavy. Emmy stays behind at the house to wait for Elle to get off the bus and Elle's teacher is on her way to get her.

On the ride there, my mom tells me it brings her joy to see me so happy. Naturally, this makes me want to pull the emotion back a little bit, there's nothing more *gay* than a boy beaming with excitement over another boy – which was *not* going to ruin my weekend.

During the ride over, the back row of seats slid loose and required being locked in. When we arrive at Gavin's house, his mom wastes no time to come out to greet us. My mom hops out and speaks to her while I go to the back seats to lock them down before I go to see Gavin. While I'm distracted, Gavin comes out, waves at my mom, then rushes back inside. His mom follows to find out what he's doing that he's not ready and my mom comes to help me lock down the seats.

"*That* was Gavin?" she asks.

"I didn't see." I respond, struggling with the seat latch.

My mom makes her thinking face, lifting her chin up to the sky and scrunching her eyebrows down as she twists up her face. She saw something she wasn't sure about, so she asked. *Uhh.* "Is Gavin *gay?*"

My neck cracks from turning so fast to look at her, "*What*?!" I ask.

"Iiis heee *gay?*" she asks again, this time demonstrating a limp wrist to help illustrate the point.

"No!" I tell her, having taken some offense to her question. It upset me because... well... because I just got the damn idea out of my head, and now my mom had to reinsert it? *Ugh!*

"*Oookkkkaaay*" she blurts, but I know what that means for my mom. It's another way of saying, *yeah, sure.*

"Why would I lie about it, mom? I don't think he is." I ask, finally getting the seat latch to work properly and locking it down.

"I don't know, I just had to ask. One look at him and I wasn't sure anymore." she shared as she slammed the side door shut. "Go on inside and help him get his stuff."

Moms just have to say that one little thing that totally upsets your mood – Why?

I walked into Gavin's house, and it was like nothing had changed. It still had the same gray colored carpet, white walls and arched openings. In their living room, a large 36" TV centered in a huge entertainment center with VHS tapes and CDs displayed around it.

In the same space, an accent wall with blonde wood covering the wall adorned with family photos and keepsakes. The archway in that wall leads to another hallway and a door that *would* lead to a garage, only it was converted into Gavin's room before we were friends.

I make my way through the house and I feel right at home. I enter Gavin's room to find him sitting in front of an old computer monitor, shirtless, bathed in the light of the sun beaming through a window behind him.

He's startled as I enter his room and looks at me with a stunned stare. I'm equally caught off guard when I see him. The house hasn't changed – but he has. His hair is short, he's taller, his body is toned...; he looks... *different.*

Our eyes lock and for a moment and we scan each other up and down. Neither of us recognize the other.

He gets up and approaches me as I draw nearer to him. Our eyes stay locked and in unison as if reading each other's minds we both say, "You look... *different*."

Of course, I took this to heart in the worst way possible. *Different* is usually not a good thing for me, but coming from him...

The reaction we share moves into laughter and Gavin returns to his computer to eject a CD. He pops it out of the tray and places it in a case. "Here, I made you a mix of all the new music I've gotten into." He hands me the case, and I'm speechless as he turns away to grab a shirt, my eyes stay affixed to his golden skin, then they sweep over his face and his body until he looks back at me and smiles with a softness in his eyes I've not seen in a long time.

My eyes couldn't deny what my mind kept trapped in my gut. Gavin is my best friend, and *now* the most *handsome* boy I've ever seen, and he wants to spend his 15th birthday with me. For the first time since 4th grade, I felt a return of the butterflies to my stomach and my skin tingles at the raising up of every follicle on my body.

Shit. What have I gotten myself into?

CHAPTER 8

UNINVITED

Gavin grabs his bag and comes up to me to stand mere inches from my face. "Look, I've gotten to be as tall as you! I might get even taller!" He excitedly shows me with a hand salute from his forehead to mine. "Come on, let's go." He beckons as he brushes up against my shoulder in passing.

I follow behind him, silently releasing a huge sigh as if I had been holding my breath since I entered his room.

I didn't expect him to be so...

He physically changed so much more than I did, even his voice had changed. The hoarseness it once possessed is now diluted and softened, but the pitch is still similar.

A familiar smell hits my nose; my cologne! I pick my shirt away from my body to waft air between the fabric and my skin. My body temperature must have risen high enough to activate the cologne, which only makes it rise more now because I'm thinking about it.

Gavin looks back at me. "Oh, I hope my cologne's not bothering you. I forgot about your allergies. I probably sprayed too much, just didn't wanna stink." he giggles and I deadpan.

It was him? Wait, he's wearing the same cologne as me?

"Is it *Bod Spray*?" I ask.

"Yup, the red one." He answers with a big smile.

Sigh. I love the red one.

We get to the van and both load up in the back row.. The van is a unique situation. It was one of my great-uncle's vehicles that was customized to allow a powered wheelchair to enter and exit without assistance. All the middle seats were removed, leaving two front seats and a row of back seats.

The two front seats can easily be removed to allow a wheelchair to be in the front as either the passenger or the driver. The back seats have to be locked in on their sliding rail, but sometimes they won't stay locked in. It happens often and can feel like an frightening rollercoaster ride. The van takes off, but the back row won't move with it until the rail its on moves to catch the seats. Earlier, I was making sure they were locked in so we didn't get strangled by the seat belts when that happens.

"This is so cool." Gavin says walking up the ramp that extended from the van.

"It's a *van.*" I retort.

"Yeah, but its a *cool* van. The door automatically opened, a ramp came out, there's all this space inside, and it kind of looks like a *fat* space ship." he points out.

"Ok, I see it. So are you saying you'd want a van like this when you can drive?" I ask him sarcastically as we get situated and buckle up.

"*Uhh no.* I definitely want a *Jeep Wrangler.*" he rebuttals and my eyes light up.

"Oh my God, me too! That's my dream vehicle right now!" I burst out with excitement.

"No way. You're saying that just because I did." he tells me with a sly smile.

Nah! "Mom! What's the car I want?" I yell to her. She's a good 8-feet from us with her music blaring to tune us out. She reaches for the volume nob and turns it down.

"What's that hunny?" she says with a sort of patronizing tone.

"I *asked*... what car did I say I wanted when I can drive."

"*Oh*, a *Dod*–?" she starts and my mouth drops as Gavin starts to laugh at me. "No, no, it was a... *Jeep! A Wrangler! Right*?!" she exclaims.

"*Yes*, thank you." I answer with complete satisfaction as I turn to look Gavin in the eyes. His mouth drops open, so I reach over to push it up and close it. "Told ya."

We laugh with each other and a comfortable silence falls between us as he looks around the van, taking in all the sights. I study his eyes and his expressions. My eyes move around his face and through his hair, to the back of his head and down his neck. He's close enough that I can feel the heat radiating from his body.

I scooch away a little to give him more space, or... maybe to give *us* space. I don't want him to be uncomfortable around me, but I'm also uncomfortable with myself around him.

I feel his eyes upon me as I move away. I look out of the window. It's a good excuse – to look out of the window.

"What's the first thing you wanna do when we get there?" he asks.

"Oh, I've got a whole plan!" I list off all the activities for the weekend, and by the time we finished talking about it, we arrive at my house. My mom gets out to help Emmy with her bags and grab the cake, meanwhile I take Gavin around on a tour to show him changes I made in my room.

Elle was already picked up, so we only had a few minutes to spend at the house before we were on our way again.

"Boys!" Emmy yelled from the kitchen where she mixed her drink for the road. "Let's gooo!"

My mom was already in the van, ready to ride. Gavin and I rushed to the side door excitedly and piled in the back over top of each other. Emmy hopped in the van's passenger seat with her mixed drink in hand and looked at my mom to say, "Hit it."

My mom hit it alright. She pressed the gas pedal so hard that the seats in the back unlocked from the rail.

Gavin and I experienced the surreal moment of the van moving without us, then suddenly the seat rail caught up with the seat and it felt like we were in a g-force simulator.

"Dang, it really is like a spaceship." Gavin comments as soon as it happens.

Ooops. "Sorry boys." My mom glances at us struggling with the tightened seat belts from her take off in the back seat from the rearview mirror. She smiles and slightly giggles. We both laugh at the experience, but I lock the seat row back in at the first red light we stop at.

On the ride to Micco, Gavin and I find more crazy, unexpected similarities between us.

"Wait, when did you get into architecture?" I ask him, following a comment he made about a building we passed by.

"I've always liked it, I just rarely talk about it. I think I might want to be an architect." he answers and again, shocks me.

I want to be an architect.

"Shut up, me too!" I shout with more excitement than it probably deserved.

"Not this again", he rolls his eyes a full circle and smiles when they come back around.

"No, I'm for real. Don't make me have to prove it again." I retaliate.

"I feel like, everyone wants to be an architect." he says. "Like its one of those 'me too' things. Sometimes I like to do things or say things just to be different, ya know? Like, I wish I could change some things about myself to stand out. Maybe I'll get two different colored contacts so I can have two different eye colors."

"*What*?!" I look at him like he's crazy. "Take it from an outsider to the outsiders, being different is *not* fun. Contacts are changeable, you can always go back to being *normal*, but when you're *really* different, there is no going back. You just are and you have to live with the consequences of being what you are."

I didn't mean to snap at him, in fact I'm a little impressed by his desire to *want* to stand out. I wonder if I embraced being different would make my life any easier or any harder. If I had *him* in my life everyday, I wouldn't even care – he's damn near perfect.

He contemplates my response for a few moments and speaks up again. "You're right, but I'd still like to stand out. That's why I like you – you're just... *you*." he tells me, *so sure of his answer.*

> *Now I have something to contemplate.*
> *Am I just me, or a version of me that is acceptable enough?*
> *...Tolerated, enough?*
> *If I could change one thing...*

I flash him a smile and turn back to the window. I think about it and decide to offer something non-controversial, one thing I'd gladly give up. "But... If I could change one thing about myself. It would be my name."

"Your name? *Why*?" he asks me.

"Bruh – *Siddael* is boring. Plus I'm a *junior!* I don't even have my own unique identity, ya know? I complain to him. My mom overhears it and chimes in.

"*Hey*, you have a beautiful name, and you make it your own by being who you are!" my mom shouts from the front.

"Easy for you to say, you're not the one stuck with it." I say under my breath and see my mom's eyes glaring at me in the rearview mirror.

"I like it. It sounds better than mine." Gavin tells me. "What would you choose if you could name yourself?"

"Something cool, like Sirius or Elias." I answer with confidence. Gavin cracks up a little at my reply. "What?" I look at him confused.

"Sirius and Siddael are like, *sooo* close to the same sound." he laughs.

I roll my eyes. What about you, are you in love with your name, *Gavin*?" I ask skeptically.

"I like my name. But... there is one that fits me better, I think." he teases me..

Gavin stops short as we arrive and the excitement in Gavin's face seeps out as he sees the gates of the house. His butt lifts from the seat where both of his hands are planted firmly on the edge. He peers between the two front seats and out of the front windshield to see the house. He silently mouths his excitement, *W-O-W*!

We exit the van and Emmy unlocks the main house for us to put our stuff away. "Alright boys, its all yours!" She says as my mom and her walk over to the guest house.

Gavin and I run inside so that he can be given the grand tour. We drop our bags at the door and I show him around. His eyes stayed wide open and his mouth dropped constantly as we toured the mini-mansion.

The first stop on the tour is the master suite since it's directly to the left of the entry atrium. I approach the tall double doors of the suite with Gavin right behind me and make the announcement. "This is the master suite!" I open up the doors to reveal the suite featuring a king size bed, sitting area, and massive walk-in closet. "We'll be staying here." I tell him proudly.

We walk around the room and he explores each corner of it. We walk into the master bathroom and his eyes reflect the dazzling beauty of the aesthetics my great-aunt Sandy designed. As we step out of the master bathroom, he looks at the bed with a puzzled face. I saw the question form as it spilled from his mouth.

"So where are *we* sleeping?" he asks.

I looked around as if I were on some prank show,

"What do you mean?" I ask him back and point to the bed. "This is it, the master *bed*-room."

"Yeah, but *like*... We're sleeping *together*, in *that* bed?" he asks. I feel my ears get red hot with embarrassment.

We've slept next to each other before so why is this an issue now.?

Is he asking because I'm gay? Because... I'm out?

"Well, yeah..." I answer with hesitation. "Its a big bed. A... a *king* sized bed." I use both my arms to point out and illustrate its size. "But... I can sleep on the couch, if you're uncomfortable with that." I offer.

"*No*, I can." he fires back.

"I'm not *letting* you sleep on the couch, its your *birthday*. I want you to enjoy this." I insist.

"Ya know what, it's not time for bed anyway. Let's continue the tour." he changes the subject.

"*Ok*, moving along..." I turn and walk out into the sitting room that transitions into an open kitchen and dining room. "Here we have a seating area, great for reading, talking, and staring off into the view of the water. I like to drink my coffee here in the mornings."

"You drink coffee?!" he excitedly asks.

"*Yeah.*" I answer, a bit thrown. I've drank coffee since I was like 6-years-old, so it's not that exciting to me.

"Me *too*! I love coffee!" he tells me.

I roll my eyes this time, *Oooh*! "So cool." I sarcastically tell him and we both laugh. "I'll make you a real good cup of it in the morning." His smile edges ear-to-ear.

He's so damn adorable, I can't stand it.

Seeing him smile forces one out of me, but I try to subdue it. This kind of happiness isn't natural.

Gavin walks through the kitchen and opens up every cabinet door, exploring everything he sees. He even looks in the microwave, the oven, the fridge, and turns on the faucet as if he were an inspector and this house had just been built.

He makes his way to the dining room that features a bookshelf with books and he fingers his way across each spine, stopping and pulling books on interior design and architecture. Sandy and Richard, her husband, whom built this house, also have an affinity for the arts.

He looks over to his right and sees the living room, a large open space with a shaggy area rug and a 60" projection TV. He walks over and falls to the rug where he spreads his legs and arms out to make a *rug* angel. I laugh at the sight of him, he's experiencing so much joy in such innocent things. Seeing him in this moment calls back a fresh memory with my mom; a conversation we had after she came back from prison recently.

On one late night, she was telling me about some of the new things she learned about while in special therapies this time around. One of the focuses was on healing the inner child. She described the inner child as the being that we are before we first experience loss, heartbreak, and trauma. A being of innocence, joy, and wonder.

Most of us lose connection with our inner child, and it makes us cold and seemingly heartless towards others. We can no longer find joy in simple things, joy is corrupted by the adult world. She told me that she believed I was still connected to my inner child, though he still needs nourishment and healing through love and attention.

To be a light in this world is to be whole, or as close to it as possible. A balancing act between the child and the adult; the light and the dark. Gavin is clearly connected to his inner child, and I believe that it's those parts of us that are so well bonded and why I feel so connected to him.

I walk towards him, and look down as I tower above him. "Having fun?" I ask.

"Yeah, you should join me." he offers.

"I'm good." I tell him, but as I step away his hands wrap around my ankles.

"No. I insist." He giggles as he attempts to pull me down. I struggle to get away and fall with half of my body landing on the sofa chair just within reach for me to hit it. "Oh my God, I'm *so* sorry!" He giggles more as I turn slowly to see him.

"Ok, you're *gettin'* it." I rush over to him on my knees and straddle him as I take both his wrists in my hands and push them to the ground above his head. I look into his eyes and he stares back. A smile smoothly crosses both of our faces and I feel one of his legs cross mine, giving him leverage. He flips me over and now straddles me; a complete reversal. I laugh awkwardly, feeling totally overpowered and unsure how he flipped me over so easily.

He's much stronger than he used to be.

"What happened?" he taunts me, "I thought I was *'gettin'* it.'"

"You are, *later*. I'm saving my strength." I fein. He has me locked down and I am totally immobilized. He continues sitting on me as I struggle. A part of me wants him to stay on me, and I question if he feels the same way since he doesn't move.

"Alright, alright. I'll *let* you up." he taunts me further, hopping up and holding my hand to help me up with him. We continue the tour by heading out of the back doors to the pool.

"Here, we have a pool and a hot tub!" I point out with my hands.

Oooh! "A hot tub. That's where the magic happens." he says with a devious smirk while raising his eyebrows up and down.

"*Riiight.*" I answer back as if I'm not sure what he meant.

Hehh. I wish.

The house sits on a steep hill that leads down to the waterfront. Halfway down the hill is a platform with a swinging bench and a fish filleting station under a tiki hut.

We stop there for a moment so he can sit on the swing, then continue down to the tiki style boat house where a large pontoon boat and two wave-runners sit on each of their own lifts. Gavin walks around and explores the boat house, fishing gear, the pontoon boat, and the wave-runners.

"Do we get to take both of them out?" he asks me, leaning over the edge of the dock to place his hands on the hull of one of the wave-runners.

"No, unfortunately one of them has a bad carburetor. So we can only take out the other." I answer him.

"You wanna go now?!" He excitedly asks as he hops on the wave-runner and pretends to be driving it.

"Let me check my itinerary..." I jokingly say as I pretend to take the paper out of my pocket and watch the spirit leave his eyes. "I'm kidding! Yes! Let's do it!" I return his energy.

We race each other back up the stairs to the house and grab our bags to get our swim trunks. We go in the master suite to change, and I offer to go into the bathroom to give him his privacy. As I change, I remember a time when we were younger and I was staying at his house.

I was in his room waiting for my turn in the shower and he had just came back in wearing nothing more than a towel. I was so uncomfortable being in his room with him, knowing he was just wearing a towel, but he had a way of making *those* fears disappear.

Even naked in a towel, he started a wrestling match with me, and back then I could easily overpower him – so I emerged the victor. He got up from the ground after his loss, and his towel dropped. I turned away immediately, as if his naked body were repellant to me, but he didn't react as quickly, taking his time to pull his towel back up. I left the room, then, to go shower and remove myself from the awkward situation.

I thought I was being respectful, but how did respect for someone get tied to not looking at their naked body?

I didn't sexualize him, but I had a fear of seeing him naked. Like – it would maybe change things between us.

Where does that come from?

"I'm done!" Gavin yells to me in the bathroom.

"Took you long enough..." I sarcastically call back as I exit the bathroom.

"Hey – there's a lot of junk to put away." he chuckles, drawing attention to his crotch with both hands. My eyes are immediately drawn to it and rise up to meet his.

Oh, God.

"*Riiight.*" I fire back with more sarcasm and we both laugh. "First one there gets to drive!" I yell as I run.

"Hey! You got a..." he yells, but before his complaint leaves his mouth, I slip on the terrazzo floor right at the door way, falling on my side. He was already right behind me and pauses at the door to shoot me a smirk, "*Never mind...*"

At the boathouse I have him put on the required life vests and check the vessel for all of it's safety crap. He hops on the wave-runner and I lower it into the water. I hop on the back behind him, and we head out of the harbor towards the Indian River.

Once we are far enough from the shoreline, I tell him he can go full-throttle. He follows behind some large boats, bouncing and jumping off of their wake waves. I direct him towards Sebastian Long Point Park, where I spent most of my childhood camping in the summers.

We explore the islands and I share with him stories of friends and enemies at the park.

When we leave, its my turn to drive and Gavin sits behind me with his arms wrapped around my vest. Maybe because he wasn't used to using the rear strap, or maybe because he felt more comfortable holding onto me, but either way, it felt so good to be held... *even* two vests apart.

"Hey!" he yells to me as we fly through the water. "There's a fin behind us!"

I look behind us and see we're being tailed by a porpoise. They're like dolphins, but have a sharper looking dorsal fin and they're a darker color too – very shark like.

"Oh no!" I tell him, "Its a shark!" I perform the words with my best face of fear. Gavin looks back, then looks at me with uncertainty. He's trying to decipher if I'm being honest or not.

"What do we do?" he asks.

"Go faster" I answer as I push the throttle. We get ahead of the porpoise, just as the engine starts to sputter.

Oh shit...

Gavin hits me on the back, "Stop playing!"

I look back at him with *real* fear in my face to answer, "I'm *not*... We're running out of gas."

Gavin's face drops and he gets pale as he looks back at the fin getting closer. "*No*..." he says in a breath.

The engine totally cuts out and Gavin scooches up closer to me, holding on tighter. "What do we do?" he asks me. If it weren't for this being a real emergency, I might have enjoyed his scooch closer to me more, but in the moment, I was equally concerned. Then I remembered... as part of the safety crap, I always put a small extra gas tank in the front compartment, just in case.

"Don't worry, I got this." I tell him as the porpoise comes up near us and blows air.

Gavin swats me again, "You lied! It's a dolphin!"

"*Technically*, its a porpoise." I correct him, then chuckle.

"Do they bite?" he asks.

"I don't know, but I don't care to find out either." I answer. We wait while floating in the water for the pod of porpoises to leave the area. I carefully lean over the handlebars to open the front of the wave-runner to fetch the gas can. Gavin holds onto my vest strap as I do it so that I don't fall over. He insists I'm clumsy and needs his help.

I begin to unscrew the gas cap and Gavin attempts to scare me by acting as if something is coming up from the water. I react just as I finish unscrewing the gas cap...

Bloop!

We both hear the soft, horrifying sound of the gas cap falling into the river.

Gavin leans over my shoulder and we watch as it drifts down and disappears into the murky waters. Our eyes meet and his face immediately scrunches up as he bursts out into a belly laugh.

I'm genuinely shocked.

Normally the gas caps have a little chain to keep them connected, but someone broke the chain on this one and so, there it went.

Bloop!

"I can't believe you just dropped it." he laughs.

"I can't believe you tried to scare me while I was unscrewing it." I retaliate. "Oh my God, Aunt Sandy's gonna kill me!"

"We can tell them it was my fault. Don't worry." he offers.

"No, I wouldn't blame you like that." I tell him.

We finish filling up the tank, return the mini gas tank to the front, and crank up. Gavin leans over me to steer as I stay ducked down beneath him to hold my hands over the gas port to not allow water to get in or gas to get out.

We make it back to the wave-runner lift without any further incident. My great-aunt and uncle, Beth and Jerry, have arrived and are making their way down to the boathouse as we pull up.

"What are ya'll doin' driving it like that?" Jerry asks.

Without hesitation, Gavin stands up, points to me and excitedly says, "He got scared there might be a shark in the water and dropped the gas cap!"

"*Wow*, really?!" I react and everyone laughs at the situation.

Ha!-Ha!-Ha! I sarcastically laugh back, "That's not *exactly* how it happened."

"I don't know, sounds about right to me." Jerry responds and Gavin laughs harder.

"See, even your uncle knows. You're just clumsy, its *ok*." He teases me and I deadpan him.

"Ok, ok. I'll stop." He gets up off the wave-runner and onto the dock to activate the lift.

"I like this fella, where'd you pick him up?" Jerry asks me.

"Oh *yeah*, Hi. I'm Gavin." He introduces himself to Jerry and Beth. This is the first time they've met each other, but their interaction would have anyone believing that Gavin was part of the family.

"Nice to meet you, son. Welcome! Our place is your place and all that B.S. You're friends with that one there, so you must be somewhat descent if he likes ya." He jokes with Gavin.

"*Somewhat*." Gavin agrees. A smile worms it's way across his face as he watches me dismount the wave-runner. "I like him, too."

CHAPTER 9

CRASH INTO ME

As the sun sets, Gavin and I attempt to make a pizza, but we burn it up in the oven having gotten distracted by a conversation with Beth and Jerry, talking to us about school and life. They find our 'antics' hilarious and offer to order us some pizza instead. We humbly accept.

Emmy comes to the back patio to sit and drink and enjoy the setting sun with us. The sky blazes with purples and twilight blues that collide with pinks and fiery oranges. Reflected on the water, it seems endless. Gavin and I swim around in the pool, jumping in and hopping out over and over again. We stay there, for a moment in the water, watching the sun together as we hold ourselves up using our crossed arms to perch our heads up at the edge of the pool.

The pizza arrives and we emerge from the water to scarf down multiple slices at a time. Jerry makes numerous comments about his envy of our youth to be able to eat as much as we want and not gain any weight. We all laugh, Gavin and I enjoying all the more slices in his honor. I feel full and start to walk away as Gavin runs up next to me and knocks me back into the pool. Completely unprepared, I fall right in with a big splash. I creep up from the water to the blurry sight of Jerry giving Gavin a high-five for his exploit.

"Watch your step buddy." Gavin yells as he takes another bite of his pizza and my uncle laughs. I splash at him to ruin his slice in response, but he tosses his plate and slice to the table and jumps in on top of me. We wrestle in the water until I reach the end of my stamina and I escape his grip.

"Twice now?" he asks condescendingly. "You're gettin' weak."

Uh oh. "Sounds like a challenge." Jerry provokes us.

"Shut up, Jerry." Emmy tells him. I'm sure she has a fear that we're going to hurt each other somehow.

"Damn it, man. Ya'll got me in trouble." he shouts back to us. "Imma shut my mouth now."

I hop out of the pool and plop down into the hot tub. Gavin follows, springing out of the water, turning towards me and away from my family to make a clear adjustment to his junk, then into the tub right across from me.

Guilt smacks me for my wandering eyes.

I smile at him and move my focus past him to the darkened sky. The lights of the homes along the shoreline all begin to turn on, reflecting their glow against the water.

The air is cool and gusty, carrying a sweet aroma of night jasmine on the breeze. A tingle runs up my spine and down to my arms as I inhale deep and release a breath that feels enchanted by the magical feeling building inside of me. Gavin keeps his smile and floats to my side.

"It's so beautiful here." he states softly. "Thank you for bringing me."

My smile greets his words, *"Happy birthday*, Gavin." As

I live the moment, I know that this will be ingrained into memory for the rest of my life.

We exit the pool as mosquitoes begin to make their presence known. My family makes their exit and tells us goodnight. They're all staying together in the guest house with plans to take us out on the boat tomorrow, against my itinerary plans, but Gavin seems excited about it, so I don't mind it so much.

We shiver as the water drips from our wet, skinny bodies and we make our way to the master suite bathroom. We both dry off, and I offer him the first shower allowing me to go and clean up our wet trail.

As he showers, I unpack my bag more fully and prep my clothes for tomorrow. I have boxers to sleep in, but I don't know if I can *handle* that. I decide to wear gym shorts with them to avoid any embarrassing moments. I take out my pocket knife, my wallet, and my sunglasses and put them on the dresser, then sit on the bed and reflect on the day. I

t's only been a few hours, but I already feel like its been days. Time with Gavin seems to move slower, and it's so... perfect. I contemplate how the rest of this night is going to go as the bathroom door cracks open.

Glowing steam bellows out from the opening and flows forward with Gavin's body as he steps into the room in nothing but his towel.

This feels oddly familiar.

"It's all yours now." he tells me. "Don't slip." He giggles.

"Keep laughin'." I threaten.

"Or what? You'll get pinned again?" he retorts, and I can't say anything back but to scoff at it, grab my clothes and retreat to the bathroom.

I hear him unpacking and getting dressed from the shower. I move quickly to not waste time away from him. It's a rare occurrence to be together now, and even more so that I get him for a weekend in a place like this, I don't want to waste any time being away from him.

"Sid!" he yells through the door.

"Yeah?" I answer back.

"Do you have your permit yet?" he asks me.

"Yeah." I answer.

"Can I see it?" he asks.

"It's in my wallet." I tell him. "On the dresser."

"Cool." he answers back.

I finish up and get fully dressed in the bathroom before I exit into the bedroom.

No towel drop risks for me, especially with him.

I'm drying my hair, scrubbing it violently with my towel as I walk up to him from the side. He's sitting on the edge of the bed looking at my wallet. He turns sharply to hand me a photo he removed from it.

It's a photo of him from a few years back that I took. He's wearing a blue shirt, and a silver chain that matches his earring. The picture looked like a professional portrait, *if I do say so myself.*

"What's this?" he asks with a puzzled face.

"It's you." I answer plainly. "You don't recognize yourself?" I ask back.

"*No.* I know it's me. I *mean*, where did you get this from and why do you have it in your wallet?" he asks me with a developing look of concern on his face.

That's a new expression. I don't think I've ever seen it on him before.

His look concerns me right back. I didn't think much of it, in fact, I completely forgot it was in there. Though, it dawns on me that people probably don't carry around pictures of their best friends. At least, not teenage *boys*, anyway.

"You don't remember when I went through a photography phase with my old Olympus 35mm camera? I took pictures of *everything*, and you *loved* to be my model." I teased him.

"*Yeah, yeah*, but why do you have a picture of me in *your* wallet?" he asks me, showing more concern than before. "That's kinda *gay*, isn't it?"

I mirror the feeling and drop my smile, "Because... you're my best friend. I like to carry your picture with me as a reminder that I still have one." I get fidgety for a moment, scared that I've made a mistake by having his picture with me. It's just another part of my accessories, like my knife or glasses. Just *there*, I don't think about it until I need it.

I start to panic, causing my ears to burn hot and my heart to race.

The insensitivity of his comment stressed an important question that hadn't been a concern until this moment. Maybe he *did* change.

He remembers, I'm gay, right?

"Keep it." I offer it to him. "I mean, it's a great picture of you and if you don't like me carrying it with me, you should take it. I don't mind." I state it as cool, calm, and collected as I could.

His expression tells me that he doesn't see how uncomfortable it made me – maybe because he seems to be. Then again I can't read his mind. This is the first time we ever had any kind of discord, honestly. Over a photo of all things.

"No." he says as the smile returns to his face and he hands the picture back to me. "No... I *like* that you keep it with you. It makes me feel good." My face reacts before words can come forth, and the expression was a combination of relief, astonishment, and confusion.

'Feel good' he said. It makes him 'feel good'?
Either he's a narcissist or there's something brewing here.

He walks past me aimed at the kitchen, "I'm going to get another slice, want one?" he asks.

Uhh. "Yeah. *Suuurrreee...*" my words trail off into my confusion as I turn and watch him walk into the kitchen.

What the fuck just happened?
He knows I'm gay, why would he say something like that... to me?

I walk into the kitchen and he offers me a plate of microwaved pizza. I take it and grab a drink from the fridge. "Gavin, you want a drink?"

"Yeah, water!" he answers.

Ooohh! "Water... cause you're *healthy*." I mock him. As I grab a soda and his water.

We sit down together and eat our second dinner. He spots a board game on the bookcase that lights his eyes up. He reaches over and snatches *Connect Four* off the shelf. "Play me!" he commands.

"You just wanna beat me at everything, don't you." I look at him with disdain.

"That's what *rivals* do." he says nonchalantly as he assembles the game board.

We play a number of rounds, finding ourselves constantly one game away from beating the other. I was finally one move away from breaking our tie when Gavin looked me right in the face and opened the bottom slot to release all the tokens. Without blinking an eye, he said, "*Oh no*, they fell."

I gasp and my mouth hangs open. His hand moves to the bottom of my chin to close it, then he jumps to the living room carpet and teases me for another round of wrestling. He rolls around like a child in a ball pit, waiting for me to join him. He pauses, lifts up his head and looks at me with daring eyes.

He remembers I'm gay right?

I move toward him, and again, he takes out my ankles. He laughs, as he crawls over on top of me. "Twice, Sid?! I got you twice with the same move?!" he taunts.

"I forgot how much of a wrestling fan you are. You must have stolen these moves from *Steve Austin*." I justify my defeat as I crawl from under him and take a knee.

"Nope, this is all original." he jokes. "You're just a sucker."

I rush and pin him down again. This time, I let loose more strength and have a stronger hold on him. I smile as he squirms beneath me, our eyes locking again, but I see a different struggle beyond the obvious in his eyes. Frustration rises in his face and he yells at me, "Get off!"

My ears feel on fire again and my stomach turns as I release him immediately and retreat to the couch. He gets up and plops back down in a chair across from me.

We don't speak for several minutes as I pant to catch my breath, more so from the anxiety I feel than the wrestling match. He moves his body and wiggles back and forth to settle into some comfort. He's sweating, but we didn't exert enough energy for him to be. Especially since he's an athlete.

As I sit in the unsettling silence between us, I wonder what made him so irritated.

> *Did I fe–...*
> *Was he ge–...*
> *No... No. That must have been my imagination.*

"Hey, you wanna watch something on this big TV?" he asks me as if nothing happened.

> *What the fuck is going on here?*
> *Am I crazy?*

"*Yeah* – I grab the remote and approach him cautiously to hand it over.

"Don't be like that. I just don't like being pinned down." he says to me in response to my body language.

"*Suuurre.*" I respond, wondering why that wasn't a behavior I saw earlier in the day. "So, wrestling probably isn't something we should do if you can't *handle* it."

"I can handle it. You just *had* me..." he trails redirecting his focus to the TV.. *Oooh!* "South Park. I love this show!"

We watched TV until the very early morning hours of Saturday. When we were finally ready for sleep, we stumbled to the bedroom where he took a seat on the sides of the bed as if to see what would happen next.

I don't want to risk any further *gay* comments or outbursts from him, so I walk directly into the master suite closet and grab a pillow and some sheets. I start on my way to the couch in the corner seating area.

"What are you doing?" he asks me with some unexpected hint of annoyance in his tone.

I return the sentiment with my own question, "what do mean?"

"Why are you getting on the couch." he glares at me.

I don't want to upset him, but I also want to make it clear that he basically told me he didn't want to share a bed with me, "Earlier you were asking about sleeping arrangements and I told you I'd take the couch. That's it."

"No, I'll take the couch." he tells me as he gets up and tries to take the covers from my hands.

"Why are you giving me a hard time over this? If you take the couch from me, then I'll take the floor."

There. I win.

"*What?* You're crazy! Then I'll sleep on the floor with you." he responds.

"If you'd sleep on the floor with me, then why would you feel so uncomfortable sharing the *bed*?" I condescendingly ask.

"Cause it's a *bed*? I don't know, I wasn't thinking." He sits back down on the bed. "Sleep here, *with* me. Please." he asks me.

I thought you'd never ask.

"Only if you're gonna be cool about it, I don't want you having another outburst on me." I specify.

He nods in agreement – *ok*. I return the pillow and sheets to the closet then walk to the other side of the bed.

Gavin is still fully clothed and hops into bed. I remember when we used to just sleep in our underwear and didn't think twice about it. Now, we're so self-aware and worried about everyone else's opinions of even the most innocent situations.

He has changed.

I think to myself as I stay fully dressed and join him under the covers. We both flip around several times until we are facing each other and start to giggle.

"I was trying to not make it awkward, but I *have* to take this shirt off. It's too hot." he tells me as he sits up and flips the shirt off over his head.

"Thank God, me *too*!" I tell him, repeating the action.

"*Way* better." he says and I nod in agreement.

"Goodnight, Gavin." I say.

"Goodnight, *Clarice*..." he whispers back to me, impersonating *Hannibal Lecter*. My eyes widen, a smile slits my face, and I slowly turn away from him.

What a weirdo. I love it.

CHAPTER 10
UNDISCLOSED DESIRES

The night passes without any further occurrences. I sleep long and deep, not waking once in the night, until a beam of sunlight breaks through the sheer curtains over the windows and strikes me in the face. My eyes are assaulted by the light when they open, forcing me to flip over and face Gavin.

I close and open my eyes again to clear my vision and see his face poking out between the pillows and the comforter. He's just laying there, across from me, fully awake with his eyes wide open, *staring*.

He looks exactly like he did when we went to sleep.

Creepy.

Uhhh. "Good morning?" I hesitantly ask. I'm not sure if the look on his face is a good one or a bad one.

"Good morning!" he shouts back and springs up, his eyes not leaving me once..

"Did you sleep OK? How long have you been awake?"

"I slept great! I love this bed! It's *sooo* comfortable. And... I haven't been up long. Longer than *you*, but not long."

Uh huh. "Well... It's your birthday so I owe you a few licks." I scurry over to his side and straddle him in the bed to softly punch him in the arm as I count up from 1 to 15. He lays there and takes them as if he feels nothing. After the 15th hit, I shout, "Oh, and a pinch to grow an inch!"

His eyes open up and he rolls over as he yells back, "*No!* Not the pinch!".

We struggled, wrestling around for a few moments, until it became clear to me that he was too well guarded.

"Ok – no pinch for now, but I'll get you... *later.*" I tell him with certainty and he giggles at me. "For now, I'll make us some coffee."

"Yes, please!" he yells and collapses back in the bed.

I get up and leave the bed, making my way to the kitchen. As I pass the huge bay windows, I see my family down at the boat house prepping for our fishing trip already.

I hear Gavin literally hop out of bed as I enter the kitchen area; he's full of energy and vigor today. As he moves towards me, I watch him from the kitchen where I've uncapped the coffee can and am filling the filter with the grinds. I watch the sunlight illuminate his body when he crosses in front of the windows.

In the mornings, this house has an atmosphere in it that gives everything the light touches a glow, but today, Gavin's body absorbs it all.

How fitting for the birthday boy, he's literally a walking ray of sunshine.

He nears me in the kitchen, smiling the entire walk over as though he had something he was hiding. He comes up behind me, and reaches over and past me to grab a mug. His position and reach around was enough to make me feel flushed – I don't like it. I move quickly out of his way..

"*Woah*. Did I scare you?" he asks, surprised by my sudden movement.

"No, just getting out of your way. You look like you're up to something." I tell him as I press the coffee brew button on the machine.

"I'm not! ...And you were fine, I could reach."

"I saw, but I don't *trust* you..." I make it more awkward with a poor choice of playful words. I don't like the feelings he's stirring in me. It's making me super uncomfortable and besides, this is Gavin – my best friend, I can't...

He shrugs his shoulders and places the cup on the counter top. We stand across from each other in the kitchen, blinded by the rising sun. Yet we are still staring off into the blue, curious how the day will play out for us.

Emmy opens the front door and yells into the house for us to come and get breakfast. She's unaware that we're standing mere feet away from her.

"Boys! Come on! We made breakfast! Boys!" she yells.

"We're right here, Emmy!" I yell back. "We're coming!"

Beth pops in just behind her. "Did y'all make coffee? I can smell it!"

"Yes ma'am!" I replied.

"Would you mind fixing me a cup?" she asks.

"Go ahead and fix one for me too, Sid." Emmy adds.

Umm. "Make that three so your uncle can have some too!" Beth continues.

"Yes ma'am." I replied again.

Gavin looks at me with a huge smile that grows with each order. We had an understanding of how quickly something small becomes a task.

"Come on, I'll help you." he offers.

"Thank you."

We prepare all the coffees and walk them out into the front yard where my family has set-up an outside kitchen with foldable tables and hot plates. They've got stacks of pancakes sitting on the side with heaps of bacon and sausage next to them.

It's chilly outside, so Gavin and I quickly cross our arms over our chests to rub them and warm up.

"Almost done with the eggs, boys." My aunt says as she looks over at us and snickers. "What's wrong, ya feelin' a little cold?"

I look at her deadpan, she giggles more and points to jackets they brought sitting in the fold-up chairs. We suit up and grab plates to eat. My aunt Beth talks to Gavin for a while, learning more about him and recalling how her father was willing to drive to meet his parents and pick him so he could continue to go to LPA.

Everyone loved him to the point that sometimes it made me feel a little jealous. Gavin was practically one of the family. If he *were* gay, he'd be a perfect partner for me.

No! Shut up! Stop thinking like that!

Whereas I struggled to find my way past our initial differences, my family has adopted him upon their first meeting. They weren't like this with my *other* friends. Nearly every boy I ever introduced them to was a problem. If they liked my friend, then they hated their parents. If they liked their parents, then they felt like the friend was a bad influence. In most cases they didn't like either, especially if they weren't originally from Florida.

Gavin was a rare exception. They loved him, they loved his parents, and they made offers to keep him incorporated into my life. He was also the only friend I had that interacted with my family as if he had known them all his life. He joked with my uncle and could hold a long conversation with my aunt without any awkwardness. Best of all, he didn't feel uncomfortable after each interaction like most of my other friends.

Hehh. What other friends?

"Is he enjoying himself, Sid?" Emmy leans over to ask me as Gavin and my aunt talk.

"I think so. He's been smiling and laughing the whole time, so I'm pretty sure it's been good for him."

"Good. I like that little fella. He's been a good friend to you. *Pa...* Pa liked him too." The coffee steams up her glasses to obscure her eyes, but her tears catch the light and sparkle beneath the lenses at the mention of her late husband. "He'd have been so happy to see you boys enjoying yourselves like this."

I plant my hand on top of hers and nod my head. Tears reciprocate in my eyes automatically, and the sight of our moment catches Gavin's attention.

I see him glance more often over my way with a sort of concerned expression on his face.

"Where is..." Gavin starts to ask Beth as it dawns on him.

"He passed away a little over a year ago." She answers.

Gavin shoots a look over at me fast enough to give him whiplash, then instantly returns to the conversation with my aunt.

"I'm sorry, I *didn't*..."

"Sid, didn't tell you?" she asks.

"No. We haven't really talked much in the last year."

"Well, he probably doesn't like to talk about it, but daddy *loved* you." she confesses as her emotions build. "He'd... have been so happy to see you still in Sid's life."

Gavin smiled, but his face returned to showing concern.

Is that heartache for our loss; for Pa's death; for me?

Before Jerry could make it up from the boathouse, we finish breakfast and leave the adults outside to return to the bedroom and get dressed for our fishing trip on the boat. Even though the sun was out, the temperature was lower than yesterday, and it felt even colder than that because of the wind.

The weather wasn't ideal for wading in the water, but Gavin and I put on our swim trunks and made our way down to the boathouse anyway. Uncle Jerry had already packed up the boat and lowered it into the water. Beth and Emmy followed quickly behind us, and before long we were on the water making our way toward a bay that was particularly good for mullet fishing.

"Sid, get your net ready." Jerry yells out as we approach the shallows. "I see a school of 'em playin' just ahead, son. See if you can cover 'em."

Without conversation I strap the net to my wrist and draw in the rope to prepare for casting. Cast-netting is a full-body workout that requires upper body strength and coordination. Most people take it for granted because they only ever see people using small, lightweight nets to catch bait. In my family, we use 7-foot to 12-foot nets that can weigh as much as 30 pounds when they're wet and we catch whopping sized mullet that we call *bank loafers*.

Gavin had never seen me throw a cast net before, nor had he ever done it himself. He was intrigued by the entire process. There was a sense of pride I felt in the moment because if there was one thing I could confidently do, it was throw a net; I've practically been doing it my whole life. I don't have much to offer as something to impress anyone else, but maybe I could impress Gavin with this, something he surely couldn't conquer me in as easily as wrestling.

"There, son! Right in front of you! Let it loose!" Jerry instructed as I spotted the school, turned, and swung the lead line of the net outward.

The monofilament of the net gets tangled in the lead-line causing the net to stay in a mess of a ball as it hits the water and the fish break, jumping all around us. My eager pride turns to disappointment and embarrassment that prominently appears on my face and in my body language in such a way that Gavin, my aunt, and my great-grandmother instantly start laughing.

"What the hell was that?!" my uncle yells at me. "Are you trying to scare them into the boat instead of catching them with the net?"

Gavin laughs and without missing a beat adds in to the jabbing. "One jumped so close to the side here that I thought I might just reach out and grab it!"

"Son, you'd probably have had better luck grabbing it

than Sid catchin' any with that damn cast." my uncle continues.

"*Hey!* It's been a while!" I retort.

"Sid, you wanna let your friend give it a try?" my aunt snickers.

"*Yea*h... Let's do that." I answer and shed the rope from my arm to hand it to him. He walks up to the bow of the boat and I show him how to pull the rope in. I demonstrate how to turn and release the net from his hands and mouth, as he mimics my movements and nods to my uncle that he's ready.

"Alright boy, don't throw it like that one and we might have dinner tonight." my uncle tells Gavin. "There! In front of you!"

"*Mrighft phthere?*" Gavin mumbles through his lips with the lead-line in his teeth.

"Go on and cast the net boy, before the fish leave!" my uncle yells.

Gavin throws the net and to everyone's amazement he gets a little more than a quarter of it to open up. As the net hits the water, mullet jump from beneath its falling lead line, but some are visibly caught in the net.

"Pull it in!" Emmy yells with excitement. "Pull it in, Gavin!"

My mouth drops open, and Gavin's eyes light up as he sees his catch, but struggles to pull in the net. He slowly turns his head to slap down my pride with the biggest smile he's had yet; the kind of smile that says, 'guess I'm better at this *too*...'.

Most guys would probably get themselves caught up in a *pissing match* as a result of that look... but, what came next changed that dynamic. As Gavin emptied the fish from the net into a bucket, my uncle told him he needed to break their necks now.

"*What?*" Gavin looked disgusted.

I picked up one of the fish and demonstrated. "Look, we do this to kill them so that they don't suffer from suffocation, but also because bleeding them gets rid of the fishy taste." I explain," you straddle your index and middle fingers on the underside of the fish, each one inside a gill. Then your thumb and the lower part of your palm leverage back against the fish's head to snap the neck."

As I demonstrate, the fish's head cracks backwards and blood squirts out. Gavin's face looks like he's going to hurl.

"I *can't*. I *can't* do that. I'll catch them, but I *can't* do that." he says as he covers his mouth and makes barfing noises.

"*Sisssssy.*" Jerry calls out.

...And the king is returned to his throne.

My uncle drops us off with two 7-foot nets at the shore to see which of us can pull in the most fish for supper. Gavin follows me, trudging along as if he were walking on land. I stop and educate him on the *stingray shuffle*, a walking technique that requires us to slide your feet to avoid stepping on a stingray and getting stung. He doesn't realize stingrays are something to fear, which causes panic to spread across his face.

"They *sting* you?" he asks with growing concern in his eyes.

"Yup. They have a barbed bone on their tail that projects poison into your body." I warned him.

"Does it hurt?" He hesitates to walk any further.

"Hell yeah it hurts! Not that I've ever been stung,

but we had to rush my great-grandfather to the hospital once for it." I highlight.

"You're lying." he accuses.

"Ask Jerry." I prod. "Go on, *ask...*"

Before Gavin could say a word, my uncle cups his hands around his mouth and yells out to us from the boat that sits about 50 feet from us in the deeper waters. "Boys! Look out, I just saw a stingray heading your way from under the boat!"

"Jerry, shut up!" Beth says as she swats at him and he giggles.

"*Nope!*" Gavin yells and he drops the net as he rushes to the shore.

"Relax, it's not here!" I yell as I retreat to grab the net and meet him at the shore. "They're not like sharks, they just swim by you."

"There are sharks here *too*?! I *can't* do it, you wi..." Gavin begins to concede to the unspoken challenge. "*Uuhh.* Let's go back to the boat."

"I *wha...*" I ask in a mocking tone. "I *what*? I didn't quite catch that."

"Jerry! I wanna come back to the boat! Can you come get us?" Gavin bypasses his concession to request safe passage, but it doesn't work that way here.

"Come on, son. Swim." Jerry yells back.

"*Swim?!*" Gavin exclaims as his panic heightens.

As much fun as it is to see him struggle for once, I feel bad about the look of fear on his face during his birthday, so I make him an offer.

"Yeah, he can't bring the boat in over here. It's too shallow. We've walked far from where we got dropped off, so we could walk back..." I offer, knowing he won't accept it because it requires walking in the water as the treeline is too thick for us to get on the land.

Gavin looks back to where we came from and notices the difficulty that the path presents. "*Nope.*"

"Then, we'll have to swim." I told him.

"I'll stay here then." he insists.

"Gavin, you can't stay here. Come on. I'll swim with you." I offer.

"Nope. I *can't*, I just *can't*." he tells me.

"Ok... What if..." I hesitate to make the offer...

But if it gets him to the boat and the look of fear evaporates to reveal his smile again, it's an offer *worth* making. "What if you *ride* on my back?"

"On your *back*? How?" he asks, not totally turned off to the idea.

"I mean, like, *piggy back*. I'll hold your legs so that most of your body can be out of the water." I offer.

"You can't swim like that." he counters.

"It's not actually deep enough that we have to swim, it'll be like chest deep. I can carry you." I confidently tell him and see the corners of his lips turning as he accepts my offer.

"Alright, but don't try to scare me!" he tells me.

"Deal."

I drop both the nets on the ground at the shoreline to come back after he's safe aboard the boat. I drop down to my knees so he can straddle my back and I can secure his legs beneath my arms. In the distance I can hear my family laughing, already guessing at what's been bargained.

I start walking toward the boat, dropping deeper down than expected into soft mud due to the extra weight, which makes Gavin a little edgy at first until I explain that it's just mud holes and *not* me trying to scare him.

We get to the boat and Gavin hops off my shoulders to be met with the same laughter and ridicule that I faced earlier at my cast-net malfunction.

"What the hell happened, son?" Jerry asks.

"I didn't wanna get stung. I didn't know there were stingrays in the water with us." Gavin answers.

"I thought you were a 4.0 like Sid. Didn't you know that there's all kinds of fish in the sea, genius?" Jerry jabs.

"Jerry, leave him alone now. If I saw a stingray for the first time I wouldn't wanna mess around in the water either." Beth saves him. "Come on, Gavin. You come sit here and have a PB&J while Sid catches dinner."

I win.

I return to the shore, collect my net, and resume fishing. With each cast, I return to the boat to bring in the fish, checking on Gavin each time to ensure that he's enjoying himself.

Things are back to how they should be now.

Gavin sits in the sun, pleasantly conversing with my aunt and great-grandmother until I finally return with his net from the shore and call it quits for the day. I caught just enough mullet to satisfy Uncle Jerry and make a skimpy dinner.

"Well, it looks like it's *fish sticks* tonight..." my uncle comments on my catch.

As we make our return, a pack of jet skiers cruise by flying into the air off the waves of boats in the channel. Gavin and I watch them, wishing we could join. He looks over to me with a suppressed smile as he mimes a reenactment of my folly dropping the gas cap. I roll my eyes and try to hold back a giggle by looking away from him. The sound that the cap made replays in my head. I feel Gavin sneak up behind me and turn to catch him.

"*Bloop!*", Gavin makes the sound as if he knew exactly what I was thinking. We both burst out laughing.

We get back to the house and help my uncle unload the boat. Once everything is pretty well removed, Gavin and I each take a handle of the cooler that contains the fish and run it up the stairs to the tiki where the swinging chair is. Emmy and Beth have set-up their fish fileting station and they immediately go to work on our fresh catch.

Since our boat chores are done, we decide to walk to the park down the road just to do something different and so he can check out the neighborhood. Many of the homes here are stunning, so we discuss the architectural details of each home that we like as we make our way to the park.

When we reach the park, it's pretty dead; just a few kids much younger than us and some teens smoking under a gazebo. We run around like two toddlers playing in the jungle gym and running up and down the towers, chasing each other. We eventually take a break by sitting on the see-saw, jumping up and down until I pause at the sight of a familiar face.

An older boy that lives next door to Aunt Sandy walks into the park and holds my attention. He's incredibly attractive, a little taller than us, with a toasted marshmallow complexion similar to Gavin's. He has long, rich, dark brown hair, and a *very* fit body. I didn't know how fit he was until now, since he appears to be visiting the park for a run on the trail... shirtless... with a six-pack.

He doesn't know me, but I've watched him from the windows for the last two summers since my aunt built this place and I've visited. Many nights I've fantasized about being down at the boathouse fishing when he suddenly appears next door on his dock, and strikes up a conversation and reveals that he's just as lonely as I am.

Sigh.

"What's up, do you know him?" Gavin asks me, noticing my gaze.

Huhh? "Oh. No. Well, yeah. *Kinda.* He's the neighbor's son." I answer back, averting my eyes.

"Oh *yeah*?" He gives a glance to the boy. "He looks kinda *gay* to me."

"You think so?!" I ask with some excitement in voice. His comment hadn't struck me as derogatory, but his follow up made it clear that it wasn't a good thing to be *gay*.

"Yeah, he looks so *girly* with his long hair and those short shorts."

"*What*?!" I look at him crossed. "You used to have long hair, too."

"Yeah, but not *that* long." He defends. "...And if I was in shape like that, I wouldn't flaunt it, ya know? He clearly wants attention."

I deadpan him. "*Attention*? I thought that was a good thing."

"It is, but for different reasons." he defends.

"Ok. Well you *keep* your reasons then. If I had a body like that, I'd be shirtless all the time. Shirts would just melt off me." I snicker at the thought.

Gavin is caught off guard by the comment and giggles too. "Like you go to put on a shirt and it just turns to liquid, *huh*?"

"Yup. Like butter on a hot pancake."

"*O-Kay*. You ready to head back? I'm gettin kinda hungry." he asks.

"*Yeah*, I guess it's about that time. I gotta get this fishy smell off of me anyway. I've got the funk of fresh caught dinner on me still." I jab at him.

"*Bloop!*" he retaliates and we both burst out laughing.

We get back to the house just in time for what might be considered a late lunch or an early dinner. The spread consists of fried mullet, cheesy grits, hushpuppies, baked beans, and mac'n'cheese all freshly prepared by my family in celebration of Gavin's birthday.

After we finish eating, my aunt comes out with a birthday cake fully lit for us to all sing happy birthday to him. He has a magnificent look of surprise on his face as we sing and he blows out the candles with the cutest grin I've yet seen on his face. We eat the cake, then chill out watching TV before it's time for us to leave back to Fort Pierce.

Beth and Jerry come to visit us one last time in the living room before they head out. My uncle took jabs at both of us for our failures throughout the day, but all in good humor. As soon as he leaves, Gavin feels the need to prove himself one last time in an impromptu wrestling match that ends in a tie with both of us panting.

We both sit on the floor, our backs against the couch, when we catch sight of *MTV Cribs* on the TV.

"I love this show! Some of the houses these celebrities have are crazy amazing. Have you seen it? He asks.

"No. I've never cared to watch how other people live honestly." I respond.

"You should watch it for the architecture then."

Ahh. "Good point."

The episode had already begun and was following the rapper, *Xzibit*, through his home. As it continues we discuss his home's interior design like what we like and what we don't. For the most part, it was like we were reading each other's minds and completely in agreement. Gavin and I had an uncanny likeness in that respect.

Then, the episode stopped following *Xzibit* and started following *Boy George*.

I know of *Boy George*, but I don't know much about him. The moment his face appears on the TV, I hear Gavin...

"Who's this *fag*?" he says with a smile.

Under totally different circumstances... no, not even then. I don't like that word. Fag, or faggot is like nigger to me. It's not a word I'll ever be ok with saying or hearing, and to hear it come from my best friend's mouth after we've practically been completing each other's sentences all weekend just feels so... foreign.

"*What'd* you say?" I ask him, wanting to clarify what I heard.

"This guy, *Boy George*. He's obviously a *faggot*, just look at him." he clarifies. "I can't believe they let people like that on TV."

I grow silent, absorbing what's happening as my friend displays a side of himself I've never seen before. All weekend, Gavin has been giving me Jekyll and Hyde vibes. One minute we're borderline romantic with each other, the next he's gay-bashing. It wasn't so prominent before this though. The hints were there, but not evident. This... this makes it evident.

The episode continues as *Boy George* tours his home and all throughout it are photographs and paintings and statues of naked men, requiring that the images be blurred for television. At one point it was as if the entire screen was blurred with just *Boy George* clearly seen amid all the censorship. It was kind of hilarious, had it not been for Gavin's alter-ego appearance we'd probably be comparing notes on his decor choices.

Gavin is absolutely mad, to the point of being upset and muttering to himself as the episode continues.

"Fuckin' ridiculous. Look at that – he's got dicks all over his house. It's *disgusting*." he scoffs.

The amount of pictured nude men *was* a bit excessive, even for my absorbent, virgin eyes – that couldn't stop watching – but this is *his* house. If Gavin were so bothered by it, he could have chosen to change the channel. It's not like *Boy George* was parading it in public... well, maybe – I have heard *gay parades* are pretty hot like that.

I continue to watch *Boy George* showcase his home while my friend becomes irrationally angrier.

He remembers I'm gay, right?

...Because he can't possibly remember that I'm gay and be making comments like this.

Gavin crawls up the chair and sits in it across from me, one leg down and the other folded up on with his foot in his hand. He leans back and looks at me to make one last comment before I decide I can't continue watching this with him.

"Honestly, I wish we could just take all the *gay* people in the world, put them on an island and blow it up. Then we wouldn't have to be bothered with them anymore." he says without so much as a thought as to how that would feel to hear as *one* of them.

He doesn't remember that I'm gay!

I feel my ears burn and my eyes water as the dagger of his betrayal slides down my chest and opens a cavity to my heart.

"Ok. I get it! You **hate** *gay* people!" I yell.

"Don't *you*?" he asks me.

"*No* – I don't hate anyone. Why would I care who someone else loves?" I answer. "Let's do something else." I suggest, scanning the room for anything that gets us out of the living room and from this eye opening episode. "Let's play *Connect Four*."

"Ready to get beat again?" he asks as if I weren't just upset at all.

Thoughts swarm me as my anxiety skyrockets. Gavin, my best friend, is *homophobic*. Since when?!

How can he not see how upset I am?
Why isn't he questioning?
How can he be oblivious to this whole situation?
Better yet, how can he have forgotten that I'm gay?!

We get into the first round and I feel my hand shake with every drop of a token. My stomach twists and urges me to vomit.

He tries to hold a conversation about the architecture of the houses in the neighborhood and *MTV Cribs*... I'm not sure, I lose interest in his words as I'm consumed by anger over his reaction to *Boy George* and his choice of words.

> *Architecture. This boy wants to talk about architecture...* amidst the chaos he just unleashed within me as if it meant nothing. Doesn't he know how *gay* architecture is?
>
> *All of the arts...* people he probably looks up to as role models in art, music, or *whatever* – some of them are *gay*. Why does it even matter? We've never talked about sex or sexuality, why does someone else's sexuality make them a target? Why are *we* targets?!

I interrupted him with targeted intent, "*Ya know*... A lot of people who work in the arts are *gay,* including architects."

"No they're not." he defends.

"*Yes... Yes they are.* Lots of famous architects, artists, and musicians are *gay*. People who changed the world and created products or music that you enjoy and benefit from. Bi, gay – all of them. Do you wanna blow them up too?"

He chuckles in disagreement, then fires a question back at me as a jab, "So what? You said *you* wanted to be an architect. Does that make you *gay*?"

CHAPTER 11
THE UNFORGIVEN

Gavin looks me in the eyes and waits for my answer. My eyes moisten as I wonder about it and what it would potentially mean for how this dream would end.

Damn, Boy George and his gay ass house. I don't care how beautiful those floors were!

If we hadn't seen this episode of MTV Cribs, things may have went very differently, but *Boy George* wasn't to blame for just being himself, nor am I.

Gavin was my anchor to the world, a person that allowed me to feel safe, loved, and comfortable. The years and strangers within them had brought influences that changed his ideologies and brought us to a very large phallic fork in the road that would dictate the future of our friendship.

His eye brows lift to ask for confirmation as his smile turns sour and I stay silent for a moment more. I sigh under my breath as I feel the answer vomit forth.

"*Ye-Yeah...*" My lip quivers.

He giggles, unsure if I'm joking or not, but then realizes that I am not giggling back. I am not smiling or waiting to give a punchline. I'm just anxiously sitting before him with the truth laid bare on this table.

"*What?*" he asks.

"*Yeah.*" I confirm again. "I'm *gay.*"

His mouth drops open and his eyes widen in disbelief.

He really did forget that I came out to him 2-years ago.

As the words tumble from my lips and climb to his ears, my great-grandmother comes into the house and yells for me. "Sid! Hunny, come take out the trash and we'll go ahead and get ready to go."

I keep my eyes fixed on his as I get up from the table. "Yes ma'am! I'm coming!" I yell back, keeping track of his eyes as I exit the house. He watches me until I am out of sight, his mouth still wide open.

I collect all the trash bags and haul them out to the trash cans at the edge of the road. I look down the street and pause to consider my options.

I could just... run away, right now.
Or maybe a car will come zooming by and just take me out of my misery.
Anything would be better than to return to the moment that awaits me.

I take my time cleaning up outside and hesitantly make my way back to the dining table to check on Gavin. He's still sitting with his mouth open and his eyes widened. It was almost comical if it weren't so telling of his headspace.

"I know you're having a hard time dealing with it right now, but we need to pack up." I tell him, my words fueled by anger and pain.

"Are you *really*...?" flutters from his mouth. "*Gay?*"

"**YES**–I told you, *Gavin*. 2-years ago, I *told* you!"

"I *forgot*."

"How in the hell do you forget your friend is gay?! It's not like everyone's going around and claiming it!" I yell at him. In all the years we've been friends... we've never had a fight, not even so much as a disagreement. We're both easygoing, go-with-the-flow kind of guys that are happy and satisfied just to be present.

I inhale deep breaths to calm my heart rate. I am furious, but I also love this boy. He has been the brother I never had but needed, and in this moment... As much as it hurts me to have heard him denounce and hate people *like* me, I feel sorry for him. He looks terribly confused, and it is *still* his birthday.

"Can we walk down to the dock and talk?" I ask him, and he nods a firm *yes* with his head.

We walk down the steps without speaking, making our way to the swinging chair where we both plop down. I lean forward to console my cramping stomach while he leans back with a dazed look on his face.

"I can't believe it," he says softly.

"*2-years ago*," I firmly remind him. "I called you, and told you, and you said you loved me no matter what, so *what happened*?"

"I *forgot*," he reiterates. "I mean, I *knew* I had a gay friend. I remembered that *someone* was gay, but I didn't think it was you."

"I don't see how you could really just forget something like that." I continue,"but also, like, I'm pretty *obviously* gay..."

"You're not *obviously* gay..." he cuts me off, but I continue.

"And *even if* I wasn't, what happened to you in the past two years that – the boy who loves everyone – has become the boy who hates *gay* people?"

We swing for a few minutes while he considers his answer, then he finally breaks the silence, "I don't know. Friends I guess."

"*Friends?*" I ask. "I'm your friend and I didn't ask you to hate on anyone."

"Some guys I hang out with now, they just don't like gay people. They say they're the reason for a lot of problems in our society. They say that they rape kids, lead people from God, and corrupt people. My friends convinced me that gay people turn straight people gay." he further explains.

Wow. That's a lot to unpack, but what's more shocking than the brainwashing is that Gavin is not the type of person to be a blind follower. He's a leader. *What happened*, Gavin?

"We can *turn* straight people gay?" I chuckle. "*I wish.* If that were the case, don't you think we'd have *infected* everyone by now just to stop the hate? Don't you think I'd have a boyfriend and wouldn't be so lonely?"

He giggles. "*Maybe.* I don't know." He sits silent again as we rock a little more and he finally begins to speak his mind more, expressing his disbelief in the fact that he was with a gay guy for the last two days. "I can't believe it. We *wrestled...* we *shared* a bed... we played in the pool *together...* I *rode* on your back." he recalls our weekend activities with discord.

Each account alienating the moments we innocently shared together, confirming my fears and reminding me why I was afraid to ever be playful or physical with another guy since my friend Michael.

"*What* about it?" I ask pointedly.

"I can't believe I did all those things with someone gay and didn't know."

"Gavin, *gay people* aren't different other than the fact that we want romantic relationships with people of the same gender. That's it. Even though I told you *years ago...* You wouldn't have known because you've never asked. We *never* talk about girls, or boys.

It's not really a part of our friendship, which is what makes this such a good friendship. Outside influences never mattered before. Not until now. I can't believe that you're acting this way about it. About *me.*"

"I *know...* I'm just *not...*" Gavin started, but was interrupted by Emmy yelling for us.

"Boys, c'mon! Time to go!" she beckoned us.

Without talking, we both get up and make a final pass through the house for any items we forgot. Gavin grabs our bags from the bedroom and I quickly tidy up the game and dining room Then out the front door and headed back into reality.

Emmy hands me the keys, "Sid, you're driving." She tells me.

No! I need to finish this conversation!

I can't say no to her so I take them and hop in the driver seat. I adjust the rearview mirror to put Gavin within view. He catches my eyes looking at him as he looks at me.

"*Bloop!*" he says as a jab again and we both smile and snicker, but the moment quickly fades into the truth of the matter before us.

The sun sets as we drive home. The dark creeps into the van and is befriended by our joint silence. Emmy tries to spark a conversation several times, but she senses the tension between us and leaves us to our accord.

As we pass the street lights that line U.S. 1, their yellow-orange glow penetrates the van, revealing Gavin's eyes to me. I want to stare deep into them to know what he's thinking, and understand from them how such a perfect weekend became so twisted over one word; one idea that didn't change anything between us.

Damn, Boy George!
Damn, MTV Cribs!
Damn it, damn it, damn it all!

The same street lights reciprocate the view for Gavin. While my eyes are distracted by the road, I can see him in my peripherals staring at me.

Why?

We finally arrive at my house and he makes a phone call to his mom that he's back and ready for pick up. It won't be long before she's here, and with so many unresolved *things* to talk about.

Most importantly, us – I feel overwhelmed that so much has happened in such a short period of time without a moment to really *deal* with it. I signal a head tilt to Gavin to follow me to the porch through the glass sliding door. He nods back and complies with my request.

My house sits on a full acre of land that has a large pond that my great-grandfather dug out, connected to an artesian well that keeps it full of water through a fountain, and stocked full of tilapia and other marine species. Lush vegetation surrounds it like a tropical rainforest; my family regards it as an oasis.

A path through the trees, bushes and flowers takes us to a dock he built over the pond, one of my favorite spots to visit in times of contemplation. The hypnotic sound of the water ejecting from the fountain and crashing into the pond is soothing to a troubled mind. The water surrounds us and reflects our thoughts back to us.

Gavin and I sit down on the floor of the dock and scoot to the edge to let our feet dangle with our toes just at the surface of the water. We are close to each other, the closest we've been since hours ago. The whole weekend we spent literally on each other's backs, embraced each other with love and acceptance, just to end up on opposite sides of a table over one word with little consequence to two people who love each other beyond its meaning.

Gay.

A fish pops up and nips at Gavin's foot in the dark and he snatches his feet up. "You don't have *stingrays* in here too, do you?" He rearranges himself to sit on his butt with both legs folded up against his chest, wrapped by his arms.

I giggle at his reaction. "No, of course not. They're minnows. They won't sting you. They just nip at you." I half-heartedly smile. "Not *everything* in the water is out to hurt you."

He glares at me, then smiles again. "*Bloop!*" We laugh, and soften our eyes at one another. Mosquitoes begin to invade the moment as they always do, and we both hop up and swat at them on our bodies.

"Let's go back to my room" I suggest, and he nods to follow.

As we walk off the dock, Gavin speaks to me lightly.

"*I...*" He starts, then stumbles on the words. "*I...* I'm not sure *what* I am, *anymore.*"

I look back at him as he manages the thought into words and I am taken with shock and surprise. His eyes are glistening with water and light trapped behind an invisible veil of pressure, fear, and uncertainty.

I am so caught off guard that it doesn't register in my mind what exactly he meant. I hear his words and my thoughts begin zooming all over the place, but they ultimately land on one fearful thought that emerged from our earlier conversation.

The idea that gay people *turn* straight people *gay* invades me and tints this experience as a different mood. As we walk back to my room, I ponder my response to Gavin's confession.

We enter the house and quickly bypass Emmy to avoid any further delays in this very intense conversation. We enter my room and Gavin sits on the bottom bunk bed. I grab and roll over the computer desk chair to sit in front of him. I don't want him to feel uncomfortable or pressured by my proximity. Gavin looks at me with a haphazard smile and I feel the words form in me, steeped in frustration and misguided by fear.

"What do you mean, you're not sure *what* you are?" I ask to confirm.

Gavin's eyes get red and his voice cracks. "I'm *not*. I'm not sure *that* I'm..." His eyes swell with water and his face turns red as his lips quiver and he releases his deepest confession to me.

He begins to cry.

"I don't *know* if I'm *straight*."

He bursts out in tears, cupping his face with his hands, and sobbing at the release of the truth of his words.

In the wake of it, I am petrified.

I sit face-to-face with someone I love deeply and he's telling me he *might* be gay, but *wasn't* sure. I wanted so badly to explore those feelings with him, but a stronger part of me considered all of the previous interactions of the weekend and saw two stories...

Gavin and I were either *falling* in love; he developed romantic feelings over the weekend that he probably wrote off until they were made legitimate upon realizing that I'm gay and meant more could transpire between us...

Or, Gavin and I share so much in common, and have for so long, that his identity is in some way tangled in mine, causing him to feel insecure about his own sexuality in review of the perfect companionship we share, most likely in contrast to his other friends. Since he has become a follower, maybe I'm just another leader guiding him down another path, and *these* aren't his own feelings, *but mine*.

Either way, I fear my actions in this moment will appear as manipulation to him, whether now or in hindsight. I desperately want to be beside him, to hug him, to hold him, to tell him I love him no matter what, to be all the things to him that he was to me for so long...

But fear... It suppresses the best expressions of ourselves in lieu of safety. So what do I do?

"I don't think you're *gay*," I tell him.

"I think we have so much in common that you're *confused* about it. Hours ago you hated gay people, and now you think you might be one? I don't think so." I negate his words and his truth.

Before any further words could come from my mouth, Emmy walks into the room in response to Gavin's sobbing.

"Boys, what happened?" She asks us, but neither of us respond. "Sid?"

"We had a *misunderstanding*." I replied coldly.

"This doesn't seem like a *misunderstanding*." She sits beside Gavin and pulls him into her arms to comfort him. Jealousy sweeps across my heart, and my internal frustration percolates into a stream of my own tears. "Hunny, your mom is here. I came in to get you, but I hate for you to leave the house feeling like you do."

"No, it's ok. I'm *ok*." He tells her as he dries his eyes on his shirt and begins to stand up. She stands with him and kisses him on the cheek. I cower to the sight. I am *capable* of love, too – but to enact it is to be a monster of manipulation and indoctrination in the eyes of society.

I hate *this world. It's so unfair.*

"Sid, walk him to the door, hunny?" she asks me.

"Yes, ma'am." I hop up and follow Gavin through the house. He picks up his bag at the door where his mom meets us as we open it.

"Hey boys!" she greets us as Gavin hugs her.

"Did you have fun, hunny?" she asks as she looks into his face and sees his eyes are red. A moment of concern crosses her face, but she quickly hides it.

"Yeah, it was amazing, mom." he answers.

"Great! Well, we've gotta get going so I can pick up stuff for your paintball event tomorrow. Oh, did you invite Sid?" she reminds him.

"I completely forgot about it," Gavin says.

He probably did if he forgot I was gay...

"Tomorrow afternoon some of my friends are coming over and we're playing paintball on one of the empty lots in my neighborhood. Do you wanna join us?" His request seems genuine, despite the prompting from his mom.

"Yeah, that sounds fun." I respond, but secretly dread.

If these are the same friends that convinced him that *gay* people turn straight people gay, then they're bound to *love* me. A part of me instantly looks forward to being able to shoot them in a non-lethal, but gloriously painful way.

"Cool, I'll call you tomorrow then." Gavin says as he walks out the door.

"Thank you again for having him!" his mom tells Emmy.

"He's always welcome here!" Emmy replies.

"Bye", I wave.

They get into their SUV and don't leave immediately. I observe them quietly from the window and Emmy joins me.

"So what happened?" she asks.

I turn to face her, but my words can't catch up to the emotions that I kept buried all weekend. From friendship, to love, to betrayal, to the sense of loss, to whatever is happening now... I sobbed.

She held me in the window without words to be exchanged between us. Moments later, Gavin and his mother leave our driveway.

"Emmy, I *think*..." I keep sobbing, "I *think* I just lost my best friend." My face scrunches up and I begin to shake as I lose my breath to the tears. "My *heart*... My *heart*... MY HEART is... *broooken*." I barely get the words out as I lose control of my body to the intense, frenzy of emotions.

"Hunny, why do you think that? It seemed like the weekend was amazing for both of you." She retorts.

"Because, he *forgot* I was gay... and he hates *us*! Then, right at the end of today, the reason why he was crying..." I try to tell her the rest of the story, but am interrupted by a phone call.

Brrring! Brrring!

Emmy leaves me to answer the phone and I hear Gavin's mom on the line. My ears perk up along with anxiety over what she'd be calling for. My mind races through thoughts of what may have happened, the worst of them being that Gavin *hurt* himself. I hop up and dry my eyes as I hurry over to Emmy on the phone.

"Hol... hold on, hunny." she tells her over the phone. "She wants to speak to you." she tells me as she hands me the phone.

A physical lump forms in the back of my throat that I can't swallow down as I take the phone to my ear.

"Hello? Sid?" Gavin's mom asks.

"Hey, I'm here." I answer.

"Hey hunny, *listen...* Gavin got in the car and had a complete breakdown. I asked him what happened, but he didn't want to talk about it immediately. I haven't seen my son cry in a long time, ya know, so I was obviously very concerned. He eventually wanted to talk about it on the drive, and he told me what happened between you two."

The lump stays in the back of my throat making it hard to breathe. Anxiety ravages my stomach as bubbles form and explode throughout my abdomen. The voice of his mom becomes distant as I listen and have a harder time hearing her. It's as if my ears are ringing, but I don't hear the tones.

Gavin's mom continues, "I just want you to know that I love you and support you. I'm not sure where he stands on it. I asked him if he had any reservations about his own sexuality, but he said no. Still, he's pretty shook up over it, so I don't know. I just wanted you to know that I understand your struggle, and I'm there for you, hunny, ok?"

I *whispered, "Yes, ma'am."* It's all I could manage to say.

My body shook, and I felt the withdrawal of everything I held sacred in Gavin, begin.

"Ok. Well have a goodnight, and thank you again for giving Gavin such a good birthday weekend."

"Good... night." I whimper as I return to tears at the click of the **END CALL** button.

I retreat to my bedroom for the rest of the night. Emmy enters and leaves to check in on me, but I don't move or leave. I just stay on my bed, crying into my pillow, falling asleep off and on. Each heartbeat widening and deepening old scars made fresh again, all of which pale to the new ones forming.

Before she goes to bed, Emmy visits my room again and sits on the bed, placing her hand on my back as I sob.

"Hunny, do you know for sure that it's over?" she asks.

"No" I answer, "But I'm pretty good at judging these things."

"Then, give it time." she offers as advice. "Anyone can come back around with enough time." Her hand pats my back and she leans over to kiss my salty cheeks.

The entire night I am unable to sleep decently. The weekend replays over and over again in my mind.

I miss him. I didn't know how much I missed him until he was present in my life again. Everything about him makes my life better. My thoughts turn sharply away from the splendor of springing love to the treason of his words.

Damn Boy George!
It's not your fault, but it is.
I don't even know any of your songs.

I finally hop up out of bed and go to my computer desk to look up music by *Boy George* on *Limewire*. I want to know if his music was worth the sacrifice I made to defend him, though I knew it wasn't really about *Boy George*, or defending anyone. It was about standing up for myself, for being different, and asking someone I love to not spread hate and violence.

A song titled, *Do You Really Want to Hurt Me?* appears several times available for download. I download the song and start to listen to it. My eyes instantly roll as my skepticism grows over my choice of fights to pick.

I see Gavin's CD gleaming light from the outside pouch of my duffel bag. I walk over and pick it up to listen to it instead. Many of the songs belong to the *Red Hot Chili Peppers*. My mom used to listen to them a lot.

I never cared for them personally, but I find their music growing on me the more I listen throughout the night. Then the tears begin to flow again, and while the music plays, I cry myself to sleep for the final time tonight.

CHAPTER 12
KRWLNG

I wake up later than normal, feeling groggy and highly irritable. I don't have the same energy I usually do, the kind that enables me to hop up right out of bed with a smile on to greet the day and invite the customary challenges that await me. Instead, I am lethargic and unexcited about the day.

Yesterday left me with so many questions. I wish Gavin had stayed one more night so we could hash it all out, but...

Oh yeah!

I remember that today he had a paintball party. I mull over if he'll actually call me about the party today or not while I roll around in bed to find a comfortable spot. I flip and turn my pillow around to find that one small patch of fabric that isn't damp so I can comfortably rest my head. I stare at the bottom of the top bunk, reaching my hand out to touch the metal bars that hold the bed above me. I imagine they're Gavin's arm in his moment of vulnerability.

I should have held him.
I should have told him I'm here for him, no matter what.

My eyes pile water on like stacks of hay, well above the threshold of a barrel to hold them.

I should have been a stronger friend.
I'm sorry, Gavin.
I failed you.
I loved you, and I failed you.

The water from my ducts burn my eyes as they dampen the last patch of dry space on my pillow.

My hand falls to the bed helplessly as a reflection of my internal condition. Helpless, hopeless, and miserably alive. I continue ruminating like this in my bed for hours until Emmy finally interrupts my self loathing to see if I want breakfast.

"Sid?" she asks as she cracks open the door.

"Yes ma'am?" I answer.

"You want some pancakes, hunny?"

The thought of pancakes reminds me of our morning together. It was only yesterday, but it feels like forever ago. I keep crying as I answer, "*Yesss, pleeaaassse.*"

"Hunny, you *can't* stay like this ok? Why don't you come on out and give him a call?" She invites me to change my situation.

"*Yeah.*" I agree, wiping my face clean. "I'll come out in a few minutes."

"Ok. I'll get started on your breakfast." She says as she leaves from the door.

It takes me a while to roll out of the bed and get to my closet to dress for the day, but I manage to make it happen. I mope out of my room and hear Emmy on the phone with my mom. I can't make out the words, I'm way groggier than usual for being awake this long, but I can tell she updated her on what happened.

"I'm up." I inform Emmy. "I'm going to the dock."

"Ok, it'll just be a few minutes now."

I open the door to a cloudy day. The overcast featured dark bottomed clouds, the kind that breed thunderstorms. It makes me wonder if his paintball party will happen or not. Then I wonder why I should even care, since I won't be a part of it. My eyes are burning hot from all the crying while I pilgrimage to the dock for communion with the water.

Sitting at the edge draws back memories from last night; Gavin's revelation. I lay down on the dock and close my eyes. My face looking upwards to the overshadowed sun.

I speak to myself and God, "God, why? Why am I here again? Please. Please, don't take him away from me." I raise my arm and drop my forearm onto my face to shield me from the sharp light that penetrates a passing cloud. The sun's rays strike my skin and warm my body.

The air is cold, and a light wind whisks across the pond sending chills up my spine. I'm just prolonging the inevitable by not confronting him. I lift myself up, and stand from the dock's uneven wooden deck. With conviction to just end the turmoil of not knowing, I grab the phone outside and dial Gavin's number.

Brrring! Brrring!

I pace around on the porch as I nervously debate my words. My hands shake as they hold the phone to my head.

Emmy opens the porch door. "Sid! Breakfast is re–" she stops herself short seeing that I am on the phone, then whispers instead. "Breakfast is ready for you." She closes the door to return to the kitchen as I continue to pace.

Brrring! Brrring!

I should just hang up. He said he'd call me, right?

Brrring! Brrring!

Ya know what... He's probably avoiding m...

The phone stops ringing, prompting me to instantly hold my breath. Someone picks up the line.

"Hello?" Gavin answers the phone, but his voice conveys a twinge of annoyance in it.

Does he know it's me already?

I wasn't prepared for it to be him immediately; my heart is beating in the back of my throat now.

"*Hellooo?*" he asks again.

The greeting stumbles from my mouth. "*Hey...*" I answered back to him. "It's... It's *me*."

"*Oh.* Hey." he returns.

"I didn't want to bother you too early, but since I didn't know what time your paintball thing was supposed to be happening, I thought I'd just call and ask."

That's it. Play it cool like him.

"Sid..." Gavin begins. "The weekend was a lot of fun, and I really appreciate everything you and your family did for me, but... I don't think we should continue being friends."

"*What*?"

"I don't hate you, for being gay. But it's not something that I believe in. I'm *Christian*..."

"So *am* I, Gavin!"

"Well, I don't believe it's natural, and I don't want it in my life. I'm sorry."

"Gavin, *wait*..."

"*Goodbye* Sid."

Click. Eeh Eeh Eeeeh.

He hung up on me. No. I can't believe it.

I dial his number again and the phone rings.

Brrring. Brrring... Brrring. Brrring... Brrring. Br...

Click. Eeh Eeh Eeeeeh.

He picked up AND he hung up on me?!

Brrring. Brr...

"Hello, is this Sid?" Gavin's mom answered the phone this time.

"*Yes*, I'm calling for Gavin." I reply with politeness hiding the indignation that I feel.

"Hunny – Sid. He already told you his choice, *didn't* he?" she explains to me. Tears well up in my eyes, refreshing the burns that had subsided during the adrenaline rush brought on by speaking to him.

"Yes, he did, but... *but why?*" I choke on the words with a shattered voice. "*Why* is that his answer?"

"I know this is hard to hear, and I hate that this isn't working out for you because you're a good kid, but he made a choice to not associate with anyone gay because it's not something he wants in his life, sweetie." She tries to console me.

She may as well follow up with telling me, 'don't take it personal', as if it's completely not. This is personal.

"I understand that, but he..." and then she cut me off.

"There's really nothing more to be said, sweetie. I love you and I wish you all the best. *Goodbye.*"

Click. Eeh Eeh Eeeeeh.

Present Day

Michelle and Becca pause walking to blow their noses and wipe the tears from their eyes. Elle and Nico are slightly ahead of us and they slow down, hearing the blowing noses.

My best friend – ever, someone I loved like a brother – my anchor in the world – *abandoned* me.

I fell to my knees on the porch that day – just dropped right to the ground – sobbing inconsolably.

My mom had just arrived at the house when I did. She came out to the porch to check on me and found me there, blubbering on the ground. Emmy came out to join us, and they both wrapped their arms around me to let me cry as loud as I needed until my pain worked its way out of me.

I was so dehydrated that the tears could no longer stream, and my throat was so hoarse that it hurt to let out even the tiniest of a sound. They rocked me between them, and comforted me with sounds like *Shhh Shhh* to soothe my aching heart in a moment of change that would forever define an era of my life.

The following week I stayed low and depressed at school. I didn't talk to anyone, I didn't smile... Honestly, I just didn't want to *exist* anymore.

"It's heartbreaking, right?" Elle asks the two women.

"Heartbreaking?! That's an understatement if ever I heard one." Michelle replies. "That boy was a down right *asshole*, and... clearly *in love* with your brother."

Becca drops her hands from her nose and shoots Michelle a dirty look, but it quickly twists into a sorrowful tearjerker movement to break eye contact.

"*He was an asshole*. For *that*, he was. Gay, straight, whatever – you don't abandon the people you love like that. If that's what religion has brought to us, then we're in terrible shape, 'cause NONE of us are perfect, or am I wrong?" Michelle defends her statement.

Becca nods in agreement, "No. You're *right*." She wipes her tears. "Alright Sid, bring it home for us. Our walk is almost over and you're still in your early teens in this story." she points out.

Elle and Nico turn around and start walking as we follow. We're nearly to the foot of the bridge, returning to the mainland with a short walk from there to our cars. As promised, I'm giving Becca and Michelle the full-story to understand the artwork's meaning to me, then she'll tell me why it was worth $10,000.00 to her at a less than stellar auction where other buyers didn't see it worth even $200.00.

The wind invigorates me as we walk, a stir of cool wind whips around and takes my emotions back to their state of being induced by Gavin. I think about him often, his name is still a part of my daily vocabulary even though he chose to discontinue our friendship and I haven't spoken to him in over two decades.

"My mom and Emmy were worried about me because I had attempted suicide once when I was younger. It was around the time that I was 10-years-old and first encountering romantic feelings for that other boy, Michael. They didn't know I was having feelings like that, or that I attempted suicide until I was about 13 and my mom found and read my journal."

"Jesus, Sid. You've got my eyes burning *enough* already, don't you?" Michelle states.

"Sorry, I know. *Believe* me – I lived it." I tell her. "They ended up not letting me stay to myself very much because of it. For the next few weeks, they kept a close watch on me and spent more time with me than they normally would have.

The result of this was that my mom and I formed deeper bonds, and I didn't discount all the music she was constantly trying to get me to listen to. She re-introduced me to *Linkin Park*, which I instantly loved the second time around; *Metallica*, and many other alternative and metal bands that I didn't commiserate with before. Some of them were on the CD that Gavin gave me.

Ironically, she was telling me a story about the lead singer of the *Red Hot Chili Peppers* coming out as bi-sexual. I don't know if it was true or not, but I wanted so badly to rub it in Gavin's face.

In the aftermath of his departure, I went to my first concert, which happened to be *Metallica* and *Linkin Park*, and in my solitude I rediscovered my joy for art. I ended up dedicating most of my spare time to it, which earned me achievements in my classes like student of the year or exhibition wins.

In a sort of sad way, I have him to thank for that. The emotional state that he triggered within me allowed for my skills to artistically layer emotions and meaning, visually. Our story, though he may deny it or not even *remember* it, was so emotionally stacked and culturally complex that it continues to inspire and drive me today.

I admit, I've tried to reach out to him several times, but I always either fall short of following through with it or I... run away. Once, I remember, in my 20s, I was working in a store and I *felt* him enter the building. I almost have a sixth sense about him, like I know when he's near.

I know, it sounds crazy, but there I was doing my job, then suddenly I feel my throat drop into my stomach and as I look over, he passes by and looks right at me."

"Did he say anything?" Becca asks me.

"No. He smirked, but he always had a smile on, so I figured maybe he didn't recognize me. I wouldn't say I had a *glow up*, but I certainly don't look like the same boy that he grew up with. Anyway, I dashed out before he had enough time to know he was even looking at a person. He basically saw the shadow image left behind in my haste to flee his sight. I can't handle being around him and not being *ok* with him.

There's a part of me that wants to run into him and pretend like nothing has changed. I'd like to think that life has shown him that it's ok to have friends that are diverse in beliefs."

"Or that it's ok to be *gay*..." Elle interjects.

"Or bi, or trans, or a gender bender..." Nico adds. "Or *a-sexual*" he says and glances at Elle.

Mmm Ha Ha! "The jury's still out on that one." Elle jokes.

"Right. I feel like we keep repeating this same issue about sexuality and gender. There are so many exceptions, possibilities, and reasons... all of it human reasoning and synthesis, which utterly equates to nothing because meaning belongs to the beholder that assigns it. It's subjective. Anything subjective is nothing to hate someone over, and certainly nothing to end lives over." I add.

"What's not subjective is the pain that those choices cause." Nico speaks with tears in his eyes. "Sid, *loved* him..."

"*Nico*..." I urge him to calm down.

"No, it's important! They want to know *who he is*, don't they?" Nico insists.

"Yeah, *but*..." I counter and fall short.

He's right.

"Well. You *loved* him, and the *ghost* of that love still haunts you. Sid creates artwork and writes stories, and does ALL OF THIS to *release* himself from the hold of that old love and those connections still possess over him. It's been 20 mother-fuck-ing years, and *that* boy is still in pain over it. He's scared people will call him a stalker, or obsessive, or what the fuck ever. But let me ask ya'll something." Nico has dropped his smile, and clearly becomes agitated by my lack of complete transparency. He now urges for more impactful words.

"When someone dies that you care about, do people judge you for *wasting your grief* on them? No. Do they tell you to get over it and move on with your life? Hell no! And why not? Because you FUCK-ING loved them. And Sid, loved... *Gavin*" Nico catches himself nearly forgetting his name.

"All he wanted to do was love him, in whatever capacity he could. Shit – he's still *loving* him, even if *Gavin* isn't loving him back. What I've learned and am most grateful for from Sid, more than anyone else I've known in my life, is what *true, unconditional love* looks like – and here in America, we are fed this *bullshit* lie about it.

It doesn't fit all neat and pretty in your life box decorated with bullshit instagram posts of pretend happiness. It lives, and it breathes, and it bleeds because until the day we die – it *survives*." Nico breaks out into tears and hugs me. "I'm sorry Sid, it had to be said."

"It's ok Nico. I appreciate you saying what I can't. *Thank you.*"

...And that is why I married him.

Elle starts slow clapping and Michelle and Becca join in. Nico giggles and gives a curtsey.

"*Wow*. I didn't know you had it in ya, Nico. You never fail to unexpectedly impress me." Elle tells him.

"*Thank you*? I think?" he replies.

I return to finishing out my story for Becca and Michelle. "In the decades that followed, I felt like I was always there in the background of his life, sending him light and love. This year, great-grandmother, Emmy, died and her death prompted me to seek closure for old wounds, the deepest of which reside there, under his name."

"Ah, hunny, I'm sorry." Michelle says as she leans in to give me a hug.

"Me *too*, Sid. I'm sorry for your loss." Becca says. "It's never easy to lose a parent, I don't care how old you are."

"Thank you... Like I was saying, in light of her death I thought it's time to let go and move on. As Nico so firmly stated, I've been churning out pieces emotionally charged and motivationally fueled by the era in my life consumed by Gavin.

What you bought tonight, *Culture Rebel*, is composed of imagery, colors, and visualized emotions from our time together. It's like you purchased a combination of the best and the worst of my memories, a visual documentary of someone that matters very much to me that I once also mattered to. There really isn't much more to tell than that. He *was* someone I loved, lost in a moment I deeply regret."

We continue walking and reach the end of the bridge. Most of the people that were fishing on the pier below have now left as the night has gotten late. Sirens echo in the distance as an ambulance and a firetruck barrel past us from the mainland headed to South Hutchinson Island.

The lights from the trucks flash and reflect off the many surfaces at the base of the bridge, illuminating everyone's faces while alternating with darkened, dramatic silhouettes. The air is now saturated with the scent of an ocean breeze that carries an undercurrent of dead fish from bait left behind by the fisherman. You can taste the salt in the air, it's thick around us, but the decaying bait certainly dissuade breathing it in through your mouth.

Nico and Elle slide down the side of the steep hill from the base of the bridge to the sidewalk that will lead us to the night's end. Michelle and Becca follow, with Nico and Elle on standby below them in case they need to be *helped* down. I am the last to reach the sidewalk.

"Well, ladies. I hope the story was what you had wished for, 'cause that's it."

"It was an incredible story. It *should* be a movie." Michelle says.

"If you know any producers, I'm open to retelling it." I chuckle.

Hha-ha! Becca gives a brief laugh before asking more. "I'm overwhelmed to be *a part* of your story..." she pauses as she puts her tissues away and fumbles around for her keys. Elle and Nico give her a kind of half cocked glance. "By purchasing this visualized memory from your life."

"Thank you." I told her. "*Now*, it's your turn."

Michelle shoots Becca a look, and Becca looks at me with confusion. "*What do you mean?*"

"The *deal* was that I'd tell you the whole story if you agreed to tell me what caught your interest in it. *Remember*?" I point out and ask, firmly.

"*Ah. Right.* Well, sweetie, I'm not really sure it'll be *that* interesting to you." she tells me.

"Of course it is!" I correct her and begin a performance of words to coerce her feelings out. "It seemed like you had a deep interest in it, dare I say, a *connection*, to it. In my experience, for something so personal to me to have some significance to you... well, that's *uncanny*. I'd like to understand it so I can learn from it."

"Ok, ok..I'll tell you. A deal's a deal, right?" She pauses to take her small tissues out again from her handbag. I haven't actually said this out loud yet." She begins to sniffle, and tears form in her eyes.

I instantly regret pushing her to divulge her interest.

"But... we came here tonight because I haven't left my house in weeks." She starts fidgeting with her fingers, and Michelle moves closer to her, placing her hands on her shoulders.

"Becca, you *really* don't have to do this, hun." Michelle tells her.

"No, Michelle. *I do.* At some point I've got to be able to say it, and it might as well be here and now." Becca states with balled up fists at her side. She's trying to hold back her emotions as they grip her body in anger.

I know that feeling all too well.

"Alright. I hear ya." Michelle confirms. "Go on then."

"When Michelle told you that *her son* died... that was a *half* truth. She didn't want to put me out on the spot because I haven't been able to bring myself to really talk about it openly yet. But you've shared so much tonight and I feel... *ready* to return the favor." Becca reveals as we all fall silent, captivated by her story. Not even a breath is heard between us as she unveils her reason for being there at the fundraiser tonight and buying *Culture Rebel*.

"The boy that died wasn't Michelle's son. He was her *son-in-law*... He was *muh... my* son."

CHAPTER 13

FAR FROM HEAVEN

A massive, audible *gasp* is expressed by the group in response to Becca's disclosure. She begins to sob uncontrollably, eliciting the comfort and love that only another mother can offer. Michelle hugs her tight and takes Becca's right hand with hers as she runs her left hand in circles on Becca's back. Becca catches her breath and takes out her tissues to dot her cheeks and eyes, while she continues.

"About 5-months ago, just after his 35th birthday... *my son..* took his own life." She barely manages to express the words as she fights to hold herself from falling into an uncontrollable release of tears. "He had three beautiful children… and…" She looks at Michelle, who drops Becca's hand and begins to dot her own cheeks and eyes. "…a beautiful, loving, and compassionate wife."

She looks at us again and we see a tint of frustration run across her face. "He had… everything, *really*. He was a blessed boy. He had no debts, he had present parents, he had a nice house… He wanted for *nothing*…" she pauses.

"But, I guess that's not true, is it? He did want *something*… or *need* something that none of us understood." She leaves Michelle's arms and walks around gesturing her emotions, speaking with her hands to illustrate her words, showing us her meaning. "He never *came out*… and said it, but he was *unhappy* with his life. *Dissatisfied* – is maybe a better word for it. It appeared in everything he did, but not in any kind of obvious way. It was small, subtle, indiscernible to anyone that didn't know him. *Really* know him.

I *thought* I did.

I *thought* I knew what real joy looked like on my son's face. I knew when he felt pain, and when he pretended to be in pain. *Hehh* – like when your kid wants to play hooky from school with a fake stomach ache, and you *know* they're faking it, versus when they're heartbroken, and don't even know how to tell you what's wrong. Well, my son was heartbroken. He was *heartbroken*, and I *failed* him."

"Becca, no you didn't. Stop thinking that." Michelle barks at her. "You're not responsible for every action your kid makes. Especially not this. Some things are just out of our control, hunny."

Becca looks at us with a tired expression as her lips twist up. "I know I can't control everything, or protect my kids from everything out there, but I believe that sometimes... we, as parents, exert so much control that we end up becoming the very thing that our kids need protection from." She pauses. "I'm afraid I became that for him..."

Elle and Nico glance over at me, looking for direction as to what to do in this situation. It's unclear where Becca is heading with her train of thought, and her grief is heartbreaking to all of us, but we aren't sure what we can do for her besides this...

"Yes, I totally agree." I speak to her guilt and self-pity. "I'm not a biological parent, but I have played the role of mentor to many people in my life and I've observed the sort of control you're speaking about. You feel you've wronged your son somehow by being overprotective? Tell us how."

"That's just it. I don't know. I mean, *something* must've happened to him. When he was young, he was so happy and care-free. Then he went through his teen years and like everyone else, he was just *different*, but nothing out of the ordinary. Not that anyone really ever noticed anyway; he was excellent at keeping his guard up. He kept everyone from really digging too deep into his feelings..." She looks down to fidget with her tissue and starts to drip tears from her eyes again. "*Even* me."

"How can you possibly be responsible for what someone else keeps locked away?" Nico chimes in.

"Easy." She counters, "Did you come out of the closet immediately when you realized you were gay?"

"No, *bu-*" Nico replies and is cut off by Becca.

"*Exactly*, hunny." She looks at him and points in the air with fury and pain. "Why wouldn't *you* share that with your parents, unless they made it clear they didn't accept it? ...And why didn't they accept it? Because they knew how *difficult* your life would be if you were, so they sought to *protect* you."

Elle adds to the discussion to defend Nico's point of view. "Well, yes. That's partly true. Parents may make decisions about protecting their kids that make them feel insecure about choices they make or may deter them from making said choices entirely. And yes, that may lead to being unhappy in reflection of roads untraveled, *but...* They are ultimately their own person, and recognize their individual needs and have a responsibility to themselves for the security of those needs.

> Nico is actually a great example of this. His parents were overprotective to the extent that he was basically only ever at home, school, or church. They were devout Catholics that were extremely homophobic, yet... Nico stands here before you, a man married to a man. Could Nico have ignored his natural urges to be gay? Sure, but what kind of life would that have been for him?" she pauses to bring her point back to Becca's.

"An *unhappy and dissatisfied one*, so what did *he* choose to do? He chose to accept that he was gay... albeit behind his parents back, but *GAY* none the less. Then, one day when Nico realized his parents might accept that difference within him, he shared that part of his life.

I can not fathom what you feel, having lost your son in such a terribly painful way. I can't imagine what life would be for me without my brother in it if he had lost that battle himself. What I can tell you is that your parenting is not what ultimately killed your son...

You did not kill him.

It's clear that you loved him and you were willing to open your eyes to new points of view for that love. It's *crystal* clear to me. Maybe he knew that, maybe he didn't, but he made that choice unwilling to find out. He *owed* it to himself at the very least to find out."

"Well said, Elle." Nico thanks her for her words.

Becca dries her tears, absorbing Elle's words in, as she nods in agreement and confirmation of hearing them. Elle walks over to Becca and hugs her tightly.

"As a kid, even as a young adult now, I can also say that we aren't always the best at communicating back to our parents how much we love them and appreciate them." Elle tells her with a broken voice. "I didn't have the best of parents. My dad was an asshole and my mom was and will always be a crazy teenager, but I still love them. I don't always like them, but love them, I do."

"God knows that's the truth." Michelle says. "I *often* don't like my parents, but you gotta love them. Elle, thank you for saying that. I think that she needed to hear it."

Elle smiles at Michelle and tilts her head down in acknowledgement. She backs away from Becca whom now faces Nico.

"Nico, I'm sorry if I came off as attacking you. I didn't mean it to seem like that. I also didn't mean to imply... well, I'm just sorry." Becca tells him in a calm voice.

"No worries, Becca. There were some nuggets of truth in it. To add to Elle's point, we each have our own decisions to make about the paths our lives take regardless of how we were raised. Did you do every thing exactly how your parents expected you to?"

"No, of course not." Becca answers.

"Definitely not. Still don't either." Michelle adds.

"Right?! Hell nah - we don't. We each find our own way. But you also have a point, Becca – parents definitely create *a lot* of the pressure we feel to form our identities as society prefers them to be. Sid showed me that, he showed me that a lot of the struggle and the conflict I faced... *Who am I kiddin'*, that I *still* face, are due to a battle that rages on inside of me between who I want to be and who I am told to be."

"Oh my God, yes. So true – *Amen*!" Michelle says in agreement.

Nico continues, "But, does that really make you responsible for someone choosing to take their own life?– *No*. Do we all play a role in the lives of others that influence people's choices?– *Yes*.

> In some way, we are all responsible for that kind of loss. As family, as friends, as a society, as a culture – when someone takes their own life, we *all* failed.

> No one person shoulders that blame, so I just want to emphasize that you are valid in your feelings. Even though I didn't know your son, we as a people all failed him, Becca.

> Those little details that we fail to acknowledge in a person's character, the one's that you pointed out... we all share the blame in not noticing them, or taking the moment to speak onto them and help someone come to find themselves, or love and

understand themselves in a way to prefer seeking out a satisfied life, than ending an *unhappy* one."

Nico places both of his hands on Becca's shoulder. "You alone do not shoulder that." He moves his hands to mime the action of taking the burden off of her shoulders, and moves the weight to his, pretending to be under extreme weight. "*We all do.*"

Becca snickers at the sight of him, but her small laugh turns to tears quickly. "You all are so amazing." She cries. "Thank you so much for sharing my burden."

Elle and Nico immediately look over to me again, waiting for my grand reply to this heavy topic.

As someone that has dropped to that low depth of despair before, I should have a pretty solid answer, right? Nope. I don't. I am as lost as anyone else on the subject. That's really just it, suicide is completely subjective. It's the heaviest price any of us will ever pay, but heavier must be the cost of living for it to come to pass. Anyone that has considered it did so for unique reasons that are only relevant to them and the composition that makes up their reality.

When I wanted to die, I wanted to escape rejection and isolation. As I moved forward through life, I ended up being confronted with that exact fear, and having confronted it, I found that it was... tolerable. It became all the more tolerable when I realized I was never truly alone in that suffering. Someone somewhere exists and longs for connection with me as I long for connection with them.

Of course connection is the remedy, because it was the fear of losing it that made life seem less worthy of living. Yet, the quality of those connections matter even more than the connection itself. Why else would so many people that are so well connected have committed suicide if not because they lacked a higher quality of connection than what their network could provide. Not that it's the sole reason, but for me and probably many, many others, just one person made that difference. Just one, deep and meaningful connection kept me from oblivion.

When he stepped out of my life, I thought that would be it for me. *'At least I have...'* was no longer a statement I could make. Except, while my focus stayed on him, another person was redeveloping their relationship with me and changed the outcome of having lost my best friend – *my mom*.

By improving the quality of our relationship, she supplanted him well enough that by the time he betrayed our friendship, I had just enough love to keep me anchored to this world *still*. Just enough to *not* feel disconnected.

It was because of him... that I learned the truth about relationships – no *one* individual is or should be anyone else's end all answer to life's challenges. The quality of our relationships is more important than their quantities. People come and go for seasons in our lives, and they play roles both in presence *and* in absence...

It was because of him... that I began to be granted the serenity to accept that things change, to have courage to change the things I could, and wisdom to know the difference.

It was because he left... not because he stayed.

But for all that I learned, I'd *gayly* trade it back to be looked at with his eyes softly upon me again. Life is more enjoyable when you can be innocently oblivious and happy rather than cynically observant and dispirited.

Then again... a cynical life comes into being only if you've totally lost the first real connection you ever made – the one that exists within yourself.

Your inner child.

In the moment that we change from child to adult, the child is pushed back to be protected by the emergence of the adult within us. Unfortunately, some of us neglect that child and we move forward forgetting who it was that we're meant to protect with the choices we make.

I finally have my response. "I *thii...* I *believe* that we each have within us an inner child, or the person we were before our parents, our culture, our society, our world begins to break us a part and restructure us to fit each their own needs." I gesture my hands at my heart to help illustrate my words for everyone.

"Conditioning and experiences cultivate a shadow self of the inner child that eventually emerges as our adult identity. You know, those angsty teenage years that we all laugh about, when teens do stupid things and *rebel* against their parents?" Everyone nods to show me they're still with me.

"Alright, well, that shadow self challenges the inner child for dominance, and *usually* wins. That period of instability is the battle between the emerging identity and the inner child. The victor is who we become."

"*Okaaay...*" Michelle cuts in.

"I promise I'm going somewhere with this. Stay with me." I tell her as I continue to make my point. "The adult identity was created to protect the inner child, right? That was the whole reason it started developing in the first place – to deal with situations and threats that innocent identity couldn't. It's purpose was to protect the child part of our identity from the outside influences that may or may not intentionally do harm to it.

Well, like *some* people with physical children, *some* adult identities are terrible inner parents and they may neglect their inner child, or worse, abuse them. Imagine if Nico's adult identity developed *hating gay people*, then saw traits within the inner child that it recognized (through the lens of outside influences) as gay. To protect *Nico*, the adult identity may have disconnected from the inner child, suppressing it until it's traits and characteristics were stifled. It's folly is that it killed the very thing it was created to protect, and in having done so it may go on living seeking joy and finding none, because it has a purposeless existence. We see what the death of an inner child looks like all the time. People lose their creativity and wildness, they block out emotional realities of childhood, and essentially switch into *survival mode* in order to live for comfort, happiness, and emotional camouflage.

The inner child requires attention, love, and nourishment like all children. The connection between our identities is strengthened or weakened by our choices which either preserve or deteriorate the inner child's sense of fulfillment.

A *satisfactory* life.

When we neglect the core of who we are by making choices against it, we stifle our own growth. Elle is right in that we each have a personal responsibility to seek out happiness that sustains us at the core of who we are. Nico is also right in that people influence us, both in the development of our adult identities, and in the quality of the relationships we need.

Both are necessary to cultivate the space that we need to feel safe to acknowledge our inner most selves and express our hearts to grow. When we lose those things, we fall. You might think if it doesn't kill you, you get stronger. Most of us don't get stronger, but we just go on living, broken, until we either decide not to anymore or fate removes us from existence."

I approach Becca and put my hand on her shoulder as I look her in the eyes.

"Whatever the reasons are for what he's done, we'll never know. They are likely as layered and complex as this night has unfolded itself to be.

What you *can* do. What you *must* do...

...Is *forgive* him. Because he *can't* anymore. Then, you *must* forgive yourself for the role you *also* played."

Becca cries and audibly exhales and breathes life back into all of us. She appears to have had a huge weight lifted off her shoulders, as though some glow returned to her, surrounding her.

She's on the path to recovery now, this moment right here was the catalyst for her change.

I feel it.

"I'm so sorry everyone." Becca tells the group.

"Hunny," Michelle clears her eyes with a tissue. "I can't take much more of this cryin' shit." Becca giggles. Nico and Elle burst out laughing.

We continue walking, quieted by the events that happened tonight. Each of us in our own minds reflecting on the words shared and the love expressed in such an unexpected series of situations.

The silence is broken by Becca.

"*Oh my gosh*, I didn't even finish telling you *why* your art was so important to me." she grabs at my attention.

"You've been through enough tonight, Becca. You don't have to tell me *anything* else." I convey.

"No, no. I want to – *really*. I came out tonight to this thing because, *yeah*, I wanted to get out of the house, but I also wanted to support something that would help me find meaning in his death. I thought maybe I can *give something* that will help save someone's son or daughter so that they don't have to stand in my place, ya know? Losing someone and *never understanding why* is the hardest part of all of it."

"Really, you don't have to expl–" I try to stop her, but she cuts me off.

"A deal is a deal, and you've more than kept your end of the bargain. In fact your story was the greatest gift I've received during this whole crisis." she continues as we reach the parking lot where our cars are parked.

My eyes swell up again.

> *I'm so tired of crying.*
> *I can feel where her words want to lead me, but...*
> *I don't want to follow.*

Pssst. Michelle gets Elle and Nico's attention by flashing a flask at them. Elle and Nico go to Michelle under the guise to hug her and get her phone number for future meet ups at the cider bar, but they're getting a night cap. Becca stops short of approaching the group and faces me.

"I expected to come out tonight, donate some money, hear some sad stories, and maybe share a little of my own. But I didn't expect to see *you*, and your *work*. When I looked at it, I *saw...* I *felt* him... You've *grown* so much."

I feel the lump of emotions swell and cling to the back of my throat, unable to escape.

It's just like before. Please don't! Please, just let it be...

"I saw... *Gavin* and the *love* in his eyes. I never saw eyes that loved someone as much as he loved you in that moment. *Just plain as day*, too. You two were clearly *connected*. How much you must love him, to still carry him with you – *Wow*, I envy that. I can't imagine what he must have experienced in cutting *you* and *that* kind of love out of his heart. Well... maybe *now,* I can.

Through your story, I finally understand the pain I didn't *know* was there. It's no wonder he *cried* so hard that night. That's why I had to have it, *Culture Rebel*. It was the *untold* story. The something I knew was there, but couldn't quite put my finger on. He really was such an incredibly *blessed* boy – that... *Gavin*." She tells me with a crooked smirk crawling across her face.

My face crinkles up, and my lips quiver. My eye lids try to keep back the flood, but they lose the battle. I feel as if I have been immediately transported back to that phone call on the porch.

No...

Becca places her hands on my shoulders now. My body loses it's strength, and I shrink under the weight of her hands. I look her in the eyes, but we both lose sight of each other through the shimmering ponds they form.

Becca weeps as her arms cross behind me and she embraces me.

Nooo. Not him...pleeeaaasse. Nooooo.

I join her in heartache. My lungs begin to swiftly and violently inhale and exhale rapidly. I can't keep the noises back as the lump formed in the back of my throat finally bursts forth as the sound of sad whaling escapes my heart and echoes from my lips, as we both fall to the ground.

Michelle, Elle, and Nico rush over to surround us. They huddle around us just like Emmy and my mom did years ago, holding and rocking us back and forth.

Shhh. Shhhh. "It's ok. Let it all out you two." Michelle says to us.

Becca whimpers out words holding me in her arms. "I forgive you son, my baby! I'm so sorry I didn't see it until now! I forgive you, *Craig*!"

I cry harder at the mention of his name. We continue rocking until the whaling ceases between us.

Becca sniffles and looks at me with soft, reddened eyes. "He'd have *loved* you... if he knew he *could* have." I nod my head in agreement and nearly lose control again.

We stay sat on the ground, crying in the middle of this wretched parking lot.

So far from where we started this night... It was such a beautiful night for such a heartbreaking story.

No more words exist between us.
None, but the last you left with me.

Goodbye...

THE END.

THANK YOU!

If you enjoyed reading this novel, please leave a review on Amazon. I read every review and they help new readers discover my content.

Final Thought

The world *needs* diverse stories that reveal new paths to understanding the human experience. Stories that unveil the complexities of consciousness, society, love, pain, and the all the choices that connect them. I encourage you to share your story to enlighten the world.

Above all else, *love* one another.

Love is real. Love is eternal. It's all that *really* matters.

When you leave this world – you will be remembered; you will be missed. Don't leave too soon, we still have beautiful memories to make.